. . . She was lying on her back on the narrow bench, her head crooked on a cushion, one leg bent so that the foot was on the floor. Her glasses, hung around her neck by a thick cord, seemed to catch a little yellow light, although draperies had been drawn . . .

She wasn't asleep. But she couldn't be roused. Now others noticed something odd. Somebody rolled up one of her eyelids. She had not fainted. She seemed limp. Her pulse was fast. . . .

OTHER BOOKS BY CHARLOTTE ARMSTRONG

THE CASE OF THE WEIRD SISTERS
THE INNOCENT FLOWER
THE UNSUSPECTED
THE CHOCOLATE COBWEB
MISCHIEF
THE BLACK-EYED STRANGER
CATCH-AS-CATCH-CAN
THE BETTER TO EAT YOU
DREAM OF FAIR WOMAN
THE GIRL WITH A SECRET
THE TROUBLE IN THOR

THE DREAM WALKER

Charlotte
ARMSTRONG

A BERKLEY MEDALLION BOOK
PUBLISHED BY
BERKLEY PUBLISHING CORPORATION

Published by arrangement with Coward, McCann &
Geoghegan, Inc.

SBN 425-02168-8

BERKLEY MEDALLION BOOKS are published by
Berkley Publishing Corporation
200 Madison Avenue
New York, N.Y. 10016

BERKLEY MEDALLION BOOKS ® TM 757,375

Printed in the United States of America

BERKLEY MEDALLION EDITION, MAY, 1972

CHAPTER 1

The cracks in this ceiling are too familiar. There is one like the profile of Portugal up in the corner. It makes a king with a crown; his long scraggy nose has a wart on it. I am tired of seeing first Portugal, then a king, then Portugal again. But even *I* can't read any more. I can't listen to the radio, either, and be dragged by the ears the raggedy journey over that dial one more day. Makes me feel as if I were disintegrating; the strands of order and purpose in my brain seem to be raveling out to a fuzz like a tassel.

It's a revelation to me that I can't—let me record this while I am practicing—cannot stare at the ceiling and wonder and worry and brood about life and death. I am to wait? Well? Meantime, what am I to do? How shall I be occupied?

So they brought me a tape recorder, which I think is a fine appropriate tool for telling this story. All I need do is talk. Some clever girl can punctuate and place the paragraphs later, if it turns out that I'm not able.

Yes, my voice plays back crisply, as it should after all my studying, and teaching, too. The girl will have no trouble. Will you, my dear, whoever you are?

Enough practice. I therefore (as Ben Jonson said) will begin.

This is a story you know already. But I'm convinced that it has been told the wrong way. The attack has always been the same. They've told you, first, the fantastic appearance of things; and piled up evidence of the marvelous. They have brought you up against what looked like proof of the impossible, until you were properly amazed. *Then* they say, "But of course it was nothing but a hoax and this is how it was done." And all the story-tellers run downhill. They must recapitulate. You cannot follow it. Or rather, you don't.

I guess I know as much about it as anyone in the world, having been in the thick of it, and in a position to hear what all those concerned have had to say. You'll remember me from the newspapers. *Olivia Hudson: dramatic teacher in fashionable New York City Girls' School.* You'll know my face: thinnish oval with nothing distinguished about it but high and too prominent cheek bones and one crooked eyebrow. *Olivia Hudson, 34.* Place me? I'm going to tell the whole story into this machine, the other way around. The scene *and* the backstage machinery, all as it happened.

Oh, it's called a hoax, now that it has been uncovered, but I'd rather call it a plot. A meticulously planned and almost flawlessly executed plot, with one strict purpose. It was all designed to damage one certain man.

It *has* damaged him. That's why I think, if I tell it my way and you follow it, there may be some gain.

It was the old power of the Big Lie. Even now,

Therein lies its wicked power. I hear people still saying, "Oh, I never believed that stuff *but* . . ." They are still talking. People drag out the same old saws. "More things in heaven and earth, Horatio." Also, ". . . smoke, there's fire." And some say everything didn't come out. "There must be more behind it than we know." The lie was so weird and wild that it is hard to believe in the liars. So it all makes for argument . . . talk, talk, talk . . . as anything that smacks of the supernatural makes for talk and argument. (See flying saucers.) People delight in challenging reason with the marvelous, anyhow. It's all the talk and the inevitable tinge of doubt that remains and still, I'm afraid, hurts him.

Of course, we didn't know where the plot was going. We had no idea what it was designed for. It rolled up to such a size, before we knew it had to be exposed, that our difficulty was . . . and still is . . . to explain. Who these people were and not only how but *why* they did it.

Very well then. It was a plot. There were four people and (as far as I know) only four, in the plot. And one of these worked simply for her hire.

The plot was directed against John Paul Marcus and only him. The rest was build-up.

I have the good fortune to be related to John Paul Marcus. I call him Uncle John, although he is my grandmother's brother-in-law, and the relationship is remote. He is seventy-seven years old now. He has never held political office but everyone knows he has served his country better and longer than most people alive. He is rich, having found it rather easy and not particularly important to make and keep money. He is influential, not because he is rich but because he is as alert today as when he was thirty and, by the sum of all the alert days of his long life, he is wise. This wonderful man has such balance and insight that he knows how to be steady in the dizzy dance of crises and confusions all around us. So he has been like a wise and beloved Uncle John to the entire United States of America. No use for me to go on about Marcus. You know how often men in responsible places have listened to him.

This is the man they wanted to pull down.

There were two men and two women in the plot. It was expensive. There had to be money, not so much in the execution of the plans—this was comparatively cheap—but to pay those who made and executed them. The man with the money had a motive. The man with the brains had a kind of motive, too. He was to get nearly a half a million dollars besides. The women—one with her kind of motive, and the other simply for her wages—cost, as usual, much less.

The man with the money was Raymond Pankerman. His grandfather made the money. His father used it productively and increased it fabulously, and in the endeavor lived to a healthy eighty-four. But Raymond just got it. He was a flabby creature—balding, with bad posture, with a pout to what was once a rosebud mouth. Fifty-two years old when all this began, married for the fifth time, no more successfully than the first. Childless, without occupation. He'd had a doting mother who had always thought he could pick up the business side soon enough. She didn't think there was

8

much to it. But when Papa died, at last, the great complex of industries continued to be run by men who knew better than to let Raymond throw ignorant decisions into an intricate and delicate structure that grew and changed as flexibly, in a real and fluid world, as a living tree that bends to the wind and drinks the rain. And is as perishable.

So there he was. Shut out. With the income, to be sure, but understanding nothing about its sources. Raymond's education, I can guess, was the most superficial gloss. He seemed to have nothing to do but spend money he never made.

He got to spending his money in a strange place.

Probably they flattered him. Probably *there,* he got what he thought was respect. Who knows? The money was useful to *them* for *their* purposes. Anyhow, Raymond Pankerman had bought himself a secret that sustained his tweed-scented ego when all busy men, and most women (especially his wives), found him dull and negligible.

But he had the primitive reactions of a spoiled baby. Rich and world-weary, with ringside tables and third-row seats wherever he went, fifty-two years old, who would imagine he would react like a four-year-old? "He spoiled *my* fun; I'll spoil *his.*"

It seems that John Paul Marcus, one day, one spring, said softly in the appropriate ear that it might be wise to look into the possibility that Raymond Pankerman's money was going into strange channels. This was something that rose to the top of Marcus' mind because of nothing in the world but experience. The long boiling and testing of the ingredients of life

9

were in the kettle. This suspicion rose up and became visible. He skimmed it off and offered it for what it was, a mere suspicion. And lo, when it was investigated it turned out to be the truth.

Raymond Pankerman was caught—shall I pun and say red-handed?

So the Law began to move toward the long cautious prosecution.

Now there are jackals and small men for hire who will scurry and poke about. So Raymond Pankerman *knew* (as the public, by the way, did not know) that he was in a bitter mess, he had been caught financing what amounted to a spy-ring, he was due to be dragged through the courts, he was suffering and would suffer more, he was in fact ruined, because John Paul Marcus had seen what was invisible, heard what was silent, sensed what was hidden. So, as Raymond was bound to see it (Raymond never having taken a long hard look at Raymond or anything else), Marcus, and *Marcus alone,* was to blame.

(I doubt whether Pankerman's underground playmates even knew of the plot. It was certainly not devised by them. Its objective may have pleased them. But the methods would have seemed to them the sheerest nonsense. No, it was, as far as anyone knows, a strictly private plot. For revenge.)

All right. There had to be money and there was money because Raymond Pankerman had a lot of it. But there had to be brains, too. It was no easy matter to cook up a way to damage Marcus. And this is where Kent Shaw came in.

When they met the plot was engendered. You take a

10

spoiled baby, too old to spank, with plenty of money, giving him power, and the reckless blind and angry wish to destroy that which has thwarted him and no wisdom and not much sense, either—bring him together with that other diabolical brain . . .

Kent Shaw hasn't been thought of as a brain for many a year but he was born an infant prodigy, just the same. He was one of those who got through Yale at something like fifteen. He always had a flamboyant quality that attracted attention. He burst into the theatre and, as a playwright-director in his twenties, he did some very exciting things. But somewhere along the line, Kent Shaw lost the thread. Or perhaps he never really had hold of it. He grew progressively farther and farther away from any relation to ordinary life as it is lived, day in and out, by ordinary people. So he lost emotional connection with his audiences. They didn't know what he was talking about. He ceased to excite them.

So he had a series of dreadful and even ludicrous failures. He grew desperate and denied his own convictions, and did cheap sensational things, contemptuously. And they failed. At last, he went abroad and shook the dust of crude America from his feet. But the war drove him back, 4F and miserable. He hung around New York. Sometimes his high-pitched voice snapped through radio bits. Sometimes he briefly caught onto the coattails of people flying into TV. He wrote a book that nobody bought. He wrote a second one that nobody printed. He developed a very nasty tongue. He lived in some cheap depressing den and wore shirts proudly darned to indicate both fastidiousness and poverty. He was down to earth, at last, and might have made use of his real talent, except that he, too, was a spoiled child. And bitter. He was a broken, bitter failure, at thirty-nine, and seemed to have survived himself by a hundred years.

But the brain, you see, was still in that head, the brilliant fantastical brain. Furthermore, Kent Shaw hated the whole world, and particularly, I suppose, America, which would no longer praise him or, worse, pay any attention to him at all. And he wanted money so that he could soar. *He* must have known that to pull John Paul Marcus down with a brilliant lie was blackest treason, whatever the Law would say about it. But Kent Shaw didn't care.

I will tell you how these two men met because for a long time it was a great mystery. No connection between them was apparent. Raymond Pankerman and Kent Shaw inhabited two different worlds. No witness was ever found, but the one, who had seen them together.

It happened in Mamaroneck on the 19th of August. In the midst of a heat wave. At four in the afternoon. Raymond had spent the morning sweating with his lawyers. He had spent his noon hour wrestling with the Press. He had fled to the modest apartment of a nephew of his current wife. This was in Mamaroneck, near the water, and he thought he would be hidden, and comparatively cool there. He had to be in the city the following day to hear more lawyers view his situation with deep alarm. But his flight had not been entirely successful since one young newsman in an excess of zeal had trailed along and was lurking outside the door.

12

Inside, however, Raymond was all alone.

The apartment adjoining belonged to some friends of Kent Shaw's who were on vacation and who had soft-heartedly given him their key. He had fled the heat wave. He was alone. Kent was not an alcoholic. That particular illness wasn't his. But he had a bottle of gin and some lemon and lime and the ice gave out.

Kent Shaw heard sounds next door. He opened the dumb-waiter and rapped on the door across the shaft with a broom handle. Raymond opened the door on his side. Kent asked for ice, recognized the heavy pink face that had been on front pages, introduced himself. Raymond had vaguely heard of him. I don't know the exact sequence that led to the happy thought that neither should drink alone. But Kent Shaw, who was small, only five foot six, and all skin and bones, took it into his head to climb perilously through that dumb-waiter shaft. So they joined forces.

There they were in the little apartment, unseen by anyone, and they mixed some drinks and they talked.

Raymond denied, of course, everything that was just then coming out in the papers. He was a wronged man. Kent Shaw agreed soothingly but he was not fooled. I don't know how soon Raymond spoke the magic sentence. But he did, saying, "I'd give a million dollars to pull that John Paul Marcus off his high perch."

And Kent Shaw said with a glittering eye, "For a million dollars, I will do just that." Startled, Raymond was cute enough to bargain. It ended up, a half a million for the "package."

I wish I had heard the dialogue. I can imagine Kent Shaw, who never could sit still, flashing up and down the room. I can see Raymond's jowls quiver with the desire to believe that this strange feverishly excited little man could help him to his revenge.

But what *could* they do to John Paul Marcus? You look at a man's life that is sweet and sound from the beginning, and to hurt him (unless you shoot or use a knife) you must lie. But what lie?

It was no good to try anything to do with women. Marcus was seventy-odd and it was ridiculous, and even if they could have successfully lied about women in his past, there would be no uproar. "Be a dud," Kent Shaw said. "The powder's damp. Who, in these Kinsey days, would get excited?"

It was no good to try anything to do with money either. Marcus had always had money. His business life was an open book. Besides, Kent Shaw knew as little as Raymond about business and money. They couldn't lie convincingly. They didn't know enough.

They thought of pretending that Marcus had committed a crime, a killing or a vicious assault. They had some nasty ideas. But any such scheme would require a good quota of witnesses, all of whom must lie, and they didn't dare trust too many people. For of course, it was their dream that the plot would never be discovered. No, crime was not good. The law is too tough. You need proof.

Then Kent Shaw thought of the effective lie. Marcus must be involved, as Raymond was, in treason! *This* was the lie to tell. Easier, much easier. Doubt was enough. No one could prove a negative, not even Marcus. Suspicion and appearances would be enough. Needn't prove it in a court. Taint was enough. Because such a taint would strike at his whole function, at the root of his meaning. Who (if they succeeded) would listen to Marcus, ever again? That was the one cruel way to get revenge.

Kent Shaw must have paced and bounced and talked and in the excitement both of them forgot the pretty convention that Raymond Pankerman was an innocent man.

"*You* can taint him by association," Kent Shaw cried.

And Raymond, who knew he was guilty, knew he was fallen, forgot to pretend he wasn't and resolved, then and there, that he would not fall alone.

But how could this be arranged? No good for Raymond to get up in some courtroom and simply lie. *He* was tainted and a man like Marcus couldn't be pulled down as simply as that. So there was the problem of evidence, some evidence. Forgery perhaps? Forgery isn't easy, science being what it is today, and it involved the risk of a hired expert, too. Then a suspicious meeting? Overheard talk? No way for Raymond to get at Marcus. If they met in the park it would hardly seem suspicious or secret. Especially as there was certainly no way to tempt Marcus, himself, toward any foolishness. He *wasn't* foolish and they couldn't expect him to be. And he lived surrounded by devoted people, none of whom they would dare to try to bribe. Kent Shaw thought he might use that very loyalty against the old gentleman. (The public would think they'd lie *for* him, he pointed out.) "But it has to get out, to the public," Kent Shaw said, putting his finger on the key of the plot. "It has to ring from the roof tops. Plenty of stuff ends up being filed in triplicate.

And forgotten. This bomb has got to go off in the market-place. At high noon. We have to get it around, call in the pressure, print it, talk it up. I know something about publicity, Mr. Pankerman."

Then, the glitter. "There was an idea I had once . . . It would have been a sensational publicity stunt. I never could see enough profit in it, never bothered to mention it. But I happen to know a pair of women . . ." Kent Shaw began to see the shape of the fantastic lie.

Raymond Pankerman wasn't impressed with the basic outline at first. He looked very sourly upon the supernatural element. Shied away. Felt he had been talking to a crack-pot. But Kent Shaw, pacing, talking, gesturing, wild with excitement, gradually sold him. "The one thing that *will* make talk," he said. "Of course, you are right. No sensible person is going to *believe* it. But he won't be able to *explain* it, don't you see? And there are plenty of people who will be awed and impressed and glad to believe because they wish such things could be. And they'll argue with the other kind. And it can be rigged so that the evidence falls out of this other thing, as if it were casually . . .

"It will work," Kent Shaw said, swearing whitely by whatever gods he had. "It will take time, some money but more time, and it must be perfectly done without any stupid mistakes. But it will work." Then he told Raymond what it was he, personally, must finally do and it clicked. Raymond saw the delicious irony. He tasted already the sweetness of his revenge.

They knew they would have time. Raymond was in for a long slow siege with the Law, months of it, be-

16

fore he would be entirely helpless. They roughed out the plot and discussed how the money was to be paid. They arranged another secret session together, there, in November. There would be, after that, the putting up of the stakes. In the meantime, Kent Shaw was to develop all details, prepare the script, line up the cast (many of whose members would never know they had been in a play). Raymond gave him expense money. Kent crawled back the way he had come. They swore utter secrecy. Who knows what they swore on? Blood perhaps, like Huck and Tom.

What they wanted to do was from coldest vanity—narrow and bitter and mean. But money and brains will serve any master. You don't think the deluded, emotional, immature can make an effect on the real and solid world of affairs, because you don't remember King John or Benedict Arnold or Adolf Hitler.

When Kent Shaw left the apartment that evening, his head was full, I'll warrant, of his masterpiece. He would pull off the biggest show he had ever staged and no one would ever know it. He could gloat in secret, meanwhile possessing the only tangible thing that a dirty, grubby, contemptible world really respects. The long green, the money.

Of course he had to line up the women. He could buy one. The other, he thought, would play. Kent Shaw had his outline and he could see much of the detail already. There were some contingencies he could not foresee. If he had, I wonder if it would have mattered.

CHAPTER 2

I realize that I have been cheating. Very well. I can't resist telling the first incident from the outside. I can tell it as an eyewitness. I was there.

It happened on a Sunday afternoon, the 6th day of December. Charley Ives called me, about one o'clock.

"You going down to this gathering at Cora's, cousin Ollie? In a cab, I hope?" I admitted I was. "Pick me up?"

"Oh, Charley . . ."

"You'll be going by. Why not, Teacher?"

"Because it's so much simpler for you to go in your own cab and such a nuisance in traffic," I sputtered. Charley often made me sputter. I had a deep long-seated impatience with him. I didn't *want* to pick him up.

"I'll be on the sidewalk," said he coaxingly.

"So easy to miss you . . ."

"Most unmissable fella in the world. Two o'clock sharp?"

"If you're not on the sidewalk, Charley, my boy, I'll just have to go on."

"Aw, Teacher," he said, "school's out."

I could see him grinning as if his picture had been projected on my dark green wall.

I went on getting ready. (I don't live at the school, but by myself in an apartment nearer the river. I may as well say that I live well, and not on my salary. I've always had quite a lot of money.) This was going to be a ridiculous way to spend a bright December afternoon, watching Cora Steffani's latest TV effort. But she'd asked her friends to come and view some filmed half-hour or other.

My old friend, Cora (born Stevens), was in the plot.

I can realize, now, that I never did entirely trust her. I knew she didn't mind lying, when she could see a profit in it. In fact, I suppose I knew she was pretty much a phony. But I was her friend. You don't choose a friend for his high moral integrity. You really don't. I'd known Cora so long. We'd gone to dramatic school together. We'd been young together and—if you keep in touch—that holds. Then, years ago, she'd been briefly married to my cousin, Charley Ives, and I suppose it made another bond.

I remember surveying, that afternoon, the split kind of life I was leading, since I'd been seeing so much of Cora lately. Days of earnest endeavor, doing the best I could with my girls and loving the work more than I ever admitted. (You grow shy; you don't want to be too vulnerable; and the great sin, these days, is taking yourself seriously.) So, days of good hard work, and nights and week-ends, running down to see Cora and certain other less than upright characters. Oh, I had fine friends in the theatre, too, people whose endeavor was just as earnest and far more significant than mine. But Cora and the raffish crew that turned up around her . . . Well, I had known her so long. And rascals are vivid, sometimes, and that's attractive.

Cora and I are the same age, much the same size, both brunettes. I had a bit of gray showing. Cora's black hair was blacker and glossier than ever. It was her livelihood to look as young as she could. My job would let me grow old.

We took different turns, long ago. I dropped away from Broadway. The fact is, I never really made it. Cora said I hadn't the guts and she was right. I hadn't the nerve or the skin for it. The sad thing is that, for all her courage, somehow she never really made it, either.

Cora Steffani. The name turned up once in a while but all the small parts she had played indifferently well didn't add up to very much. But she still, at thirty-four, seemed to think that, next year, she'd make it. *That* I admired. As for Cora, I knew she thought I had feebly fallen back on an unearned income and was dabbling. But she had known me so long . . .

In a way, we were each other's habit. We had a curious pact of plain speaking. We didn't have many secrets, one from the other. The secrets we did keep, each to herself, were the deep ones.

Charley Ives was on the sidewalk. He got in and *filled* the cab, the way he does. Charley is a big man and he takes space, but why does he seem to take *all* of it?

"Hi, Teach."

20

"Charley, my boy, how long have you been standing on the sidewalk?" I sputtered.

"Oh, twenty minutes."

"You could have *been* there. It was silly to wait for me and five minutes' ride."

"With contraptions like those on your feet in the dead of winter," said Charley morosely, "you're going to talk sense?" I bristled. I was wearing black satin, without so much as a button's worth of ornament on it, and it needed frivolous shoes. "Silly, she says," brooded Charley. "Lay off, or we'll fight, Cousin Ollie. I'm in no mood for this clambake, anyhow."

"Why must you go?" I said.

"Ask me no sensible questions, I'll tell you no silly lies," said Charley idiotically.

Charley Ives was Marcus' grandson, which made us more or less cousins. Long, long ago, in the days just before the second war really broke upon us, Charley and I had a fight. I don't like to remember it, but I do, clearly. I, stamping and howling that art and truth and beauty and understanding and being sensitive to people's infinite variations, all this was important, Hitler or no Hitler. Charley shouting that all that mattered—all—was to stand up with your kind and kill your enemy or be killed and dramatic art was for the birds. It was a very young and very stupid argument. Charley went to war and was gone a long time. When he came back, long after the peace, he wasn't young any more. And neither was I.

He, too, was thirty-four, that December day. He'd taken to calling me "Teacher." It made me feel elderly and stiff and ridiculous. So I called him "Charley, my boy," and God knows whether he minded.

He brought out the very worst in me. When I was with him I *was* the teacher. The stereotype, I mean. Something waspish and preachy. The truth was, he mystified and therefore irritated me.

After the wars, Charley had bought into a publishing house. (Everyone in our family seems to have money. Perhaps we bask in the golden glow around Marcus. I don't know.) But it seemed to me that Charley (of all people!) was doing no work. The money did the work, for all that I could see, and Charley was window-dressing. He was so big and he looked relaxed and knew how to be charming and he turned up everywhere seeming to have no pressing duties on his mind.

(The young woman who had shouted Hooray for art and sentiment and dainty understanding, she had learned to keep quiet. She hid in a shell that was poised and calm and she never shouted any more. But the young man who had been so willing to get killed . . . where was he?)

Charley stirred. "You going down to Washington for Marcus' birthday next month? How about flying down together?"

"I can't go until the last minute. Classes."

"I can go anytime," Charley said easily. "So it's a date."

I sat there thinking, Of course you can go anytime. Why *don't* you have something that limits you?

"What are you going to give him for a birthday present?" Charley wanted to know.

"A book," said I.

"He's got a book. I send him crates full. I had an idea. Want you to help me pick it out."

"Why me?" said I. Why fly down with *me?* I was really wondering. Why wasn't he taking Cora? I knew he had taken Cora to see Marcus, while they were married, and that Marcus hadn't cottoned to her. Marcus is ever gentle, but you are not left in doubt about his feelings. Now, I didn't know whether she and Charley Ives were engaged again or what. I thought, grimly, it was probably "or what." The fire and flame between them had died away abruptly, long ago. Yet Cora acted as if he belonged to her and Charley, amiably, let her do it. I knew Charley worshiped Marcus. For all I knew, he'd split with Cora because of Marcus. If now, at the age of thirty-four, Charley, my boy, was torn about marrying his ex-wife all over again against his grandfather's advice, he didn't confide in me. I was afraid he would. It was none of my business. I didn't understand a thing about it. I didn't want to know.

"I like your taste," Charley said. "In fact, I defer to it."

I'd lost the thread.

"Do you know you're about as absent-minded as a full professor?" Charley teased me. I didn't answer or we'd have fought.

Cora's apartment, on the fringe of the Village, had one really good room. It was full of people that day. Only two of them mattered. Kent Shaw, faintly bouncing with tension, as usual, was sitting in a corner. And Mildred Garrick was there. A large woman with a

23

cherub face, a crown of braids on her head into which she had a habit of thrusting feathers or flowers according to her fancy. Today she had a fat maroon velvet rose over her left eyebrow. Mildred wrote a column. She looked surprised to find herself where she was. And, since she could—an' she would—print one's name, Mildred was Queen-for-a-day in that company.

"Olivia, beloved," gushed she. "Do you know, the older you get, the more absolutely distinguished you become?"

"You're just being kind," I said as dryly as possible. "Do you know Charley Ives?"

"Of course. Of course. Of course." Mildred pulled me aside. "What am I doing here?" she asked me with round eyes.

"Oh, come, Mildred, don't be such a snob."

I saw Cora put one arm around Charley's neck, pull him down and kiss him on the cheek. She then sent him to tend bar and he went, wearing her lipstick.

"When is this program?" demanded Mildred. "I have an appointment . . ."

Somebody said, "It's just about two-thirty now."

Cora was wearing tight black-and-white checked pants and a black blouse. Her thick-rimmed glasses rode on her head like a tiara and the cord attached to the earpieces hung off the back of her neck. She was too busy to greet me. She knew she needn't bother. She was swaggering back and forth, hands flying, gesturing people onto cushions. "Kent, darling," she said in her affected way that by now was her only way, "is the little gadget hooked up? Kent's going to take this off on a tape for me. For the voice. Isn't he a sweet?"

I craned my neck and saw Kent fussing with a recorder. "I'm ready," he snarled, "to make you more or less immortal." Nobody bothered to resent Kent Shaw's snarls any more.

"Somebody tune in CBS, then. Now, kids, I don't say this is high holy art . . ." Cora's eyes flashed mockery at me. She suddenly crossed her legs and sank swiftly to the floor. She pulled her glasses down to position, put her elbows on her knees, pushed finger-tips into her cheeks, and was absolutely still.

The screen filled, music played, a title flashed on.

I was watching Cora's face. She was not at all a beauty. The face was thin. She had a rather long straight nose with a most distinctive tip to it. The nostrils flared back; the very tip of the nose made a sharp little bony triangle. That nose was the most arresting feature, gave all the character to her face. The effect was inquisitive and a bit mischievous. I was thinking that no make-up could change it. I was thinking, also, that Cora had this much skill. You did not know what went on in the head. The face did not need to tell you.

Somebody said, "Hey, Cora, I thought . . ."

"Oh no!" she cried tragically and clutched her forehead. "This is the wrong film! I'm not on! Oh no!"

So she rose. The slim legs were supple and strong. She got up from that cross-legged pose like a fourteen-year-old. "I'm so sorry!" she cried, desolately, and walked to the far end of the room and flung herself upon the window bench.

People exerted themselves to be good sports about the fiasco and a great hubbub arose, very loud and jolly. Even Mildred Garrick tried not to make her intention, of getting away as fast as she could, too obvious. Everyone let Cora alone, assuming she was upset and embarrassed. In the corner, the tape recorder ran, apparently forgotten.

It was Charley Ives who said quietly in my ear, "Is Cora all right, do you think?"

So I looked at her. She was lying on her back on the narrow bench, her head crooked on a cushion, one leg bent so that the foot was on the floor. Her glasses, hung around her neck by that thick cord, seemed to catch a little yellow light, although draperies had been drawn, to protect the TV screen, and where she lay, it was dim.

"Can't be asleep," I murmured. I thought Charley hesitated to go himself to rouse her or comfort her or whatever. I thought he wanted me to do it. So, of course, I went.

She wasn't asleep. But she couldn't be roused. Now others noticed something odd. Somebody rolled up one of her eyelids. She had not fainted. She seemed limp. Her pulse was fast.

People said not to crowd, to let in some air. Someone drew the curtains open and she lay, just as limp, in full daylight. Somebody wanted to call a doctor. Somebody asked what time it was. Somebody answered.

Cora opened her eyes and sat up.

Charley said, "What ails you?"

"I don't know. I went away."

"Fainted?"

"I don't know. I was walking on a beach," Cora

said in a perfectly matter-of-fact voice. "In my green summer cotton."

"Dreaming? You couldn't have been asleep."

"Wait," she said sharply. "Wait . . ." It was as if she were catching a dream back that might fade. "Josephine Crain was there. I walked up to her. I said, 'Josephine, please tell me where we are.' She doesn't know me. Then I remembered what I've read. I said, '*You* are in Florida. But where am I?' Then I was frightened. I was terrified. I walked very fast, hard to do on the sand, in my white sandals with heels . . ." Cora looked down at her feet in black heel-less slippers, and I know I shivered. "What"—she began to rub her head—"what happened?"

"Must have had a dream," said somebody soothingly. Somebody brought her a drink. Cora sat huddled together. I thought she looked all of thirty-four. "It was the strangest kind of dream," she muttered. "I think I will crawl into bed, if you will all excuse me."

"Do you feel ill?"

"I don't know."

Mildred Garrick said to me, "Now, what was all that?" She pranced out. People left, awkwardly, and at a loss for an attitude. It was just awkward, just odd. Kent Shaw waited until nearly last. "I'll leave the machine," he said. "Don't make a mistake and erase it."

"Erase what?" said Cora. "What do you mean, Kent, darling?"

"The thing was running the whole time. You might want your analyst to hear it."

"I don't want to hear it at all. Take it away."

Kent shrugged and took it away. Charley and I were left with her. He took her hands. "What happened, now . . . really?" Charley can be very sweet and gentle. Some big men can.

"Just what I said. I can't tell you more than that." She pulled her hands away. "I thought I was on a beach."

I said, "So long, you two."

But Cora said, "No. Charley, you go away. There's a dear man. Let Ollie stay with me." (We had known each other so long.)

So Charley left and I stayed. Cora didn't go to bed. We lounged, talking quietly, not about her dream or whatever it was, but gossiping a bit. Cora didn't seem to bother to put on any act for me. I thought she had suffered some queer mind-lapse and it had frightened her. I thought she was toughly assimilating whatever the sensation had been. I let her be. She finally said she felt all right. I knew she meant that I could go.

She had the grace to thank me, in a phrase that was pure Cora. "Your ivory tower has made you a nice peaceful type to have around," said Cora.

"No questions asked," I said lightly. "Have a snack and go to bed, why don't you?"

"Ollie, I will." She kissed me. Then, just as I went through the door she said, "Ollie, you know Josephine Crain, don't you?"

"Um hum."

"She *is* in Florida?"

"Miami. Yes."

"When will she be back?"

"The 20th, I think. She's going into rehearsal."

"Sometime," said Cora, "ask her."

"Ask her what?"

"If I was there."

Josephine Crain is one of our truly great. She came back to town, as planned, and the day after, right in the midst of the Christmas rush, Cora called me. "Ollie, do something for me? I know you will."

"I might if I knew what it was."

"Go and see Josephine Crain. You know what to ask her. Kent Shaw's promised to go with you."

"Oh, Lord, Cora, she's busy. I can't bother her."

"But I've got such a bad thing about her. Please. Meet Kent at the theatre. He says they are reading this morning. They'll break around two."

"Meet you and Kent Shaw?"

"Not me."

"Why not?"

"I can't go, Ollie. I'm too scared."

I was her friend, wasn't I?

Josephine Crain is a great and gracious lady. She led us into a bare dressing room, me and Kent Shaw and that tape recorder.

"Jo," I said, "I've got a funny thing to ask you. Can you remember anything about where you were or what you were doing on December the 6th, in the afternoon? Can you place it?"

"I must have been on the beach," she said. "I always am after lunch."

"Did—?"

"Wait," said Kent Shaw. "Miss Crain, may I turn this recorder on?" Jo's lovely eyebrows moved. "I want to record what you say. You'll see why." He was terribly excited, must have been. He hid it fairly well.

"Is this all right, Olivia?" Josephine had amusement in her warm rich voice. Her eyes asked what I was doing, traveling with Kent Shaw. "I'm not going to be sued, am I?"

I said, "I think perhaps it's a good idea. It will settle some foolishness. I'll explain later."

"If you say so," she smiled. So Kent Shaw plugged in the machine.

"Now, Jo," I said, "please try to remember December 6th, around about two-thirty in the afternoon. You were on the beach, you say. Did anything the least bit odd happen?"

"Odd? December 6th was a Sunday, wasn't it?"

"Yes. It was."

"What do you mean, odd, Ollie?"

"I don't want to suggest anything."

"You don't mean the woman in the green dress?" said Josephine Crain.

I was stung with surprise and then immediately by un-surprise, by suspicion. I heard Kent's breath whistle out. "Go on," I said.

"Well, that was certainly odd. This perfect stranger came plodding along. Spoke to me. Called me by name, in fact. Asked me to tell her where we were."

"What time was it? Can you quote her exactly?" *I* asked the questions. Kent Shaw didn't speak. Perhaps he didn't dare.

"It was . . . oh, middleish. Between two and three, I would say." Josephine's voice changed to one sharper and harsher than her own. " 'Josephine, please tell me where we are.' "

"What did you do?"

"I goggled, naturally. Then she said, '*You* are in Florida. But where am I?' So I said, 'You are in Florida, too, for heaven's sakes. What's the matter?' But she went away very fast. She vanished."

"Vanished?" I gasped.

"I mean, of course, she just disappeared." Jo gestured impatiently.

"*Disappeared!*"

"She left the beach, to be perfectly literal. What is the matter, Ollie? She went between two buildings to the street or so I suppose."

"Describe her, Jo?"

"Brunette. Slim. Not as nice a figure as yours, but not bad. Green cotton dress. White sandals with some kind of heel. Nothing to say about the face except a longish nose with a pulled-over flattened tip to it—"

"Oh me," I said, "oh my! You don't know a Cora Steffani, Jo?"

"No."

I reached for a clipping from an old theatre magazine. "This face?"

Josephine's eyes narrowed. "That is the nose. I don't think I'm liking this, Ollie."

"No. You won't like it," I said.

"I'll play back the other piece of tape," said Kent Shaw in his shrill voice.

Well, of course, it was all there. The time, too. Verified by the fragment of the TV program and somebody's questions. Josephine Crain didn't like it one bit. "What is this supposed to be? A trick?"

"Very like," I said, feeling stunned.

"*Yours,* Mr. Shaw?" Josephine lifted her brow, in that instant divining what we weren't to know for a long, long time.

He bared his teeth. "I think I've been used," he snarled. "I don't appreciate it."

"What made you bring that machine to Cora's?" I demanded.

"Someone had borrowed it. I'd picked it up to take home. Cora spied it and insisted." His dark face looked intent and angry. "Only how could she *know* I would have it?"

"The whole thing is ridiculous," Jo said. "If it is a trick, why? This woman is a friend of yours, Ollie?"

"Let me play the tape for Cora Steffani," I said slowly. "I'd like to see what she does about it."

"We can always erase it," said Kent Shaw boldly, and as if he had a mind to do it, then and there.

But we didn't erase it. Kent Shaw and I, and Charley Ives and Mildred Garrick (who'd heard about this somewhere) all watched Cora listen to it. Watched her cut off a scream and fall to weeping. She hung on to Charley's sleeve and wept on his jacket. She wouldn't talk. She seemed terrified. After a while, she begged *us* not to talk about it. Mildred Garrick pinched her lips together.

How could a woman be in two places at once? How could she walk in a dream? How could Cora lie on a bench in her own room surrounded by people, and walk on a beach in Florida, too? No sensible person could believe such a thing. Mildred was suspicious and had no comment.

Nothing, apparently—happened. Oh, there was some talk in Cora's little circle. Cora seemed to try to squelch it. She put the tape away. Did not destroy it. Jo Crain refused distastefully to answer questions. Nothing seemed to come of it.

Kent Shaw acted as uneasy and suspicious as anyone else. He must have been throbbing with triumph and excitement.

Because it was a brilliant beginning. Almost flawless. Josephine Crain was above suspicion. Josephine Crain needed no sensational publicity, of course not. So the incident was just odd. Hushed up and very odd.

But the tape and the unimpeachable witnesses, one of whom was myself, to prove a woman had dreamed in New York and walked in Florida—this existed.

Now I will tell you about Darlene Hite, and how she did it.

CHAPTER 3

She was the fifth child in a family of seven. (Darlene! Lord knows what they named the other six!) The family was poor. It hadn't gone in for education, either. Darlene had to meet the world on her own, with no help, financial or otherwise, from her background. She was born in San Diego, California, and she was bright and not bad looking. She left home at sixteen and made a try for the movies.

Any girl who launches herself toward any form of show business runs into difficulties. Nobody ever made it easily. If she is like Josephine Crain, *both* sensitive and tough, *both* delicate and indestructible, she isn't hurt and she makes the top. If she is like me, just sensitive, she draws away from pain, does something else. If she is like Cora, just tough, she fights tooth and claw, never admits she is hurt or a failure. If she's a Darlene Hite, she is either toughened or destroyed.

Darlene Hite never knew the world to be anything but a jungle and everything that happened to her made her think she was alone in it. She was cool and clever, but she was limited. When she needed help, she didn't know where to turn for it. So Darlene was betrayed and cheated and had no recourse. What she learned by "experience" was what she had already expected. *Darlene*, she believed, had to look out for Darlene. She was toughened.

She went to work in a third-rate nightclub, still show business, although she was only intermittently a performer, and most often a kind of Johanna Factotum. She was a lone wolf. The loneliest of wolves, living a cruelly underpaid and defensive existence with iron control, until Kent Shaw came after her.

Darlene, by this time, was thirty, a somewhat artificial blonde, but slim, medium high and gray-eyed, like Cora Steffani. Her face was not as narrow. Her eyes were, in fact, larger and lovelier. The mouth was not the same either. But the nose, the long nose with that distinctive tip to it, gave all the character to her face. And it was Cora's nose.

Kent Shaw had seen her during his Hollywood phase some years ago. Now he approached her with what must have seemed like perfect candor. He had a scheme on. She, and only she, could help him work it. Therefore, she could name her price and he expected it to be high.

Darlene listened. Wouldn't you?

It was a publicity stunt, he told her. He was going to raise a certain actress into a blaze of light. Darlene vaguely understood that this other woman had a wealthy protector who could pay. To accomplish what he had in mind, Kent Shaw said, he needed Darlene for a series of performances over a period of months, which he would devise and which must be played exactly as he directed. She was cool and clever and could do the job. But it wasn't her cleverness he wanted to

35

hire. Many girls were as clever. She, and she alone, was qualified. Because of the shape of her nose.

How much would it pay? Darlene wanted to know. He told her. Darlene did not ask if she was going to go against the law or do harm. She asked what she had to do. The money must have looked like a shaft of sunlight cutting down into the jungle. When Kent Shaw swore her to secrecy, Darlene understood that, too. In Darlene's world, secrecy was natural. Of course one kept one's business to oneself, and especially a Good Thing.

If she had known the true objective of the plot, would she have agreed to work for wages? I don't know. Maybe Darlene would not know. She had narrow horizons. The meaning of a man like Marcus might not have been visible to her, from where she struggled alone down in the dark thicket.

Kent Shaw invented the scenes, chose the costumes, picked the sets, wrote the lines, set the timing. Darlene had, as Cora had, a tiny sheaf of narrow paper slips on which, in a kind of shorthand they well understood, this script was written. Such an *aide-mémoire* was necessary. For it was a long drawn-out show. The scenes were to be played weeks apart. But time and sentences had to be exact, to the word and to the minute. Communication with the director, once the curtain went up, would be (almost) entirely cut off. Darlene hid her script in the same place Cora's was hidden, a place always close about her person, that no one ever suspected.

She got into Miami the night before the 6th of December and went to a modest rooming house, appearing quietly dressed, not too prosperous, not too young, not very interesting. She wore on her dyed-black hair a small hat with a nose veil. The veil had a fancy edge that nicely obscured the tip of her nose. She used a name that I've forgotten and implied that she had come to town to take a job and would seek permanent living quarters on the morrow.

She stayed close in the room until after noon the next day. She left, then, wearing a cloak of darkness. It was a light-weight garment, something like a duster, with loose sleeves and a belt. Darlene already had her hair piled high with a comb like Cora's but she covered this with a scarf. She walked to the quiet little hotel on the water where Josephine Crain always stayed. She went into the ladies' room and slipped out of the duster. It hung inconspicuously over her arm and hid her handbag into which went the flat-heeled dark shoes and out of which came the white sandals. Now she appeared in a duplicate of Cora's green cotton dress. In fact, she was close to a duplicate of Cora.

She walked out upon the beach and spotted Josephine. Darlene checked the time, to the minute. She was a very cool and competent person. She walked on stage, said her lines, and fled.

Going between two buildings, Darlene slipped from white to dark shoes, pulled the comb from her hair and let the hair hang to her shoulders. She was inside the duster and buttoned up in a matter of seconds. The woman who stepped into the street would not even have been shouted after by any pursuer of the woman who had left the beach. Thus, she vanished.

She went quickly back to the room, burned the first

little slip of instructions, paid her bill, left town by bus immediately. Nobody noticed her. Why would anyone?

The whole thing, of course, rested on the invariable habit of Josephine Crain, who was "always" alone under her umbrella on the beach in the early afternoons. The gamble was that she would be there on the 6th day of December. If she had not been alone, it wouldn't have mattered much. But she had to be *there*.

She was there.

Kent Shaw had done brilliant research. He chose for his unconscious cast and took his gambles on people with routine habits. They were people above suspicion and therefore of good repute. Well-known people, who had set themselves in patterns. He had combed the nation for such people. They were all middle-aged or older. They were all successful people who did as they pleased, who had developed routines which were respected. There are more of such people than you would think.

The gamble was the weakness of the plot. Ah, but when it paid off, it was the plot's wicked strength! None of these people could possibly have been bribed. Their testimony was truthful and unimpeachable.

The first incident went off beautifully.

Still, the result was meager, for all the planning and all the trouble. Why weren't they discouraged?

Kent Shaw, watching, delicately prodding in his own person the course of events, playing for the biggest stake of his life and having planned it this way, was simply absorbed. To Darlene Hite, it didn't matter. Placidly, she, the employee, could go on, win or lose, to the next part of her job. Cora Steffani was, after all, on stage, even though, so far, the stage was very small and obscure and the audience merely her own circle of quite insignificant people like me. Still she had the role and must henceforth play it to whatever audience.

But Raymond Pankerman could have seen and heard nothing at all for his money (since Kent Shaw was ruthless that they communicate in no way whatsoever). Still, Raymond was surrounded by harassments of his own. And, after all, the bulk of his investment in this strange affair was not to be paid out except for value received. The big money lay in a shabby old safe which stood in a run-down, cheap-rent, one-room office, taken in Kent Shaw's name. But Raymond held the combination to this safe. Kent Shaw couldn't get into it . . . yet. So, Raymond could afford to shrug and be patient.

There was, as I said, some talk. I remember the first *argument* I heard. One Saturday, after Christmas, I ran into Charley Ives, downtown, and he begged me to come and look at his idea for Marcus' birthday present. He took me to a jeweler's and showed me a letter cutter, gold and steel, an exquisite thing.

"It's beautiful," I said. "Of course, Marcus *has* paper cutters."

"Marcus has everything," Charley said lightly, "but a token of love is a token of love. I wasn't sure of the design."

I don't know what took me by the throat. I said to myself it was outrageous that a man, a big strong healthy intelligent man like Charley Ives should be

39

fussing over a little bit of a birthday present; should have the *time* for such fussing, however exquisite the gift or beloved the recipient.

"I know I'm no artist. What's the matter?" said Charley innocently. "I kinda like it. You tell me if it's all right, Ollie."

"*Of course*, it's all right. You *know* it's all right."

"Gosh," said Charley.

"Gosh what? Charley, my boy."

"I don't know why you're cross with me, Teacher. I'm being a good boy."

I might have blazed out at him if he hadn't turned to tell the clerk that he'd made up his mind. Then he grabbed my arm. "Don't apologize," he said cheerily. "Come on, let's have lunch."

We wheeled into the nearest restaurant and there was a man Charley knew, another big man, named Bud Gray. Somehow, this Mr. Gray attached himself and joined us and I was glad.

One of these days, Charley and I were going to have another fight. The truce between us had gone on too long. When Charley came home, at the war's end, so briefly, I was fighting the battle of Broadway, and Charley, worrying about post-war problems in Europe, had no time for mine. Besides, I avoided him, knowing and feeling guilty about it in my soul that all civilians fight a war in safe soft places. When Charley came home after his spell in occupied Germany, I was teaching. We met at Marcus' house and Charley seemed mildly surprised that I wasn't trying to be a great actress any more.

I told him, to put it simply, that I had failed. "I didn't have what it takes," I remember saying.

"What does it take?" He'd seemed amused.

"Among other things, courage," I'd told him.

Charley said to me, "Doesn't everything?"

"Cousin Charley," I'd said, "let's not fight. I withdraw the word 'courage.' Probably I don't know what it means. I know I haven't got it."

"Whereas, I'm as brave as a lion but I 'don't understand,'" Charley had said coldly. "Okay, Teacher. No fight. So be it." The truce had set in.

It wasn't long after that that he met Cora Steffani and there was fire and flame and they ran off. Two months later, she went to Reno and Charley went to Japan.

That was just as the Korean affair broke out, so he was gone again quite a long while. Then he came home and became (of all things) a publisher and we began to meet (of all places) at Cora's.

I'd seen a lot of him. (He'd seen a lot of her.) And sooner or later I was going to tell him how I thought he was wasting himself and I was going to sound like Teacher, sure enough. When I announced that I thought there was an awful lot of man to waste, when I told him to his teeth that I knew he was no boy. When I asked him why . . . why . . . why . . . was *he* hanging around, playing the play-boy?

And I didn't *want* to fight with Charley Ives again.

To get back to the restaurant . . . pretty soon Kent Shaw came in, saw me, came over to ask me how Cora was. He said he hadn't seen her in a couple of weeks

41

(and no more had he). This led to Kent's sitting down with us to wait for his date, and all of us telling Charley's friend, Bud Gray, about the strange dream or trance Cora had gone into, and how it seemed as if she had been in two places at once.

Mr. Gray said he'd call such a thing impossible because, in human experience, it was unknown.

Kent Shaw said, "That's where you're wrong. It's not unknown. What I can't swallow is that it could happen to Cora Steffani."

"When has it been known?" Charley wanted to know.

"Why, there was a Saint . . . Anthony, wasn't it? Don't remember the details, but *he* managed it. Then there was Maria Coronel. You never heard of her? A lady of Spain who would fall into such trances and wake up, claiming she'd been busy converting Indians. No doubt they thought she was off her sixteenth-century rocker. Only thing, when some Spaniards got into Mexico, somewhere, they kept hearing from the Indians about a mysterious lady in blue who had come around preaching. Point is," Kent Shaw grimaced, "such a thing happens to a saint or a religious type. *Not* to an aging and not very successful actress who has no religion at all."

I waited for Charley Ives to resent this. "You're talking in terms of miracle?" inquired Charley with an interested air.

"What else?" Kent said. "Now, if it had happened to Olivia—"

"Oh, for pity's sakes!" I said.

"I don't say you are a religious," said Kent as if he

42

apologized for calling me a dirty name, "but just the same, you've got a dedicated air about you, something as honest as the sun," said Kent Shaw solemnly (That little fake!), "a little bit out of *this* world. Whereas Cora Steffani . . ." His whole face was a sneer.

"Charley and I are both very fond of Cora," I said stiffly.

Kent Shaw drew back his lips in that smile that was so unpleasant. "Still, I think I've made my point."

Charley sat, looking at him. Charley has long tan eyelashes. He keeps his face tanned, I don't know how, and his eyes are so vivid a blue that they startle you, framed in those lashes in that browned face so near the color of his hair. Charley's not a handsome man. But he is not one that goes unnoticed. He *filled* that chair. Kent Shaw looked back, as saucy as a terrier.

"In the case of this Cora," said Mr. Gray soothingly, "at least there is evidence that isn't mere legend."

"Evidence!" scoffed Kent Shaw. "Oh sure. A tape recorder beats the word of a saint. Naturally. Naturally."

"A legend is not the same thing as a record."

Well, they argued until a newspaper man named Ned Dancer came in and Kent whistled to him. As Ned came over, Kent dropped the subject, but this Bud Gray was full of unused ammunition. "I still say," he said, "that if this Maria of yours had had a tape recorder and a flock of affidavits from those Indians, then you'd have a comparable basis."

"Affidavits!" scoffed Kent. "You can have them. I'm willing to believe in Maria Coronel because it's charming. But in Cora Steffani, I am not willing to believe."

"What was it then? Coincidence?" asked Gray. "You're willing to believe *that*?"

"Or was it prearranged?" asked Charley.

"What was *what*?" Ned Dancer wanted to know. So he was told. Perhaps he thought his leg was being pulled. He shut his mouth and refused comment. But of course, now he had heard about it.

Charley asked me, after Kent Shaw had gone, what *I* really thought. I said I tried not to think about it and I must go.

I didn't want to answer, if he asked me whether Cora was a liar. I was trying so hard to mind my own business.

The second incident happened on January 4th or January 5th, depending . . .

CHAPTER 4

Last night I stopped without finishing a sentence. I thought my voice was failing. Come now, my voice will not fail if I use it properly and I can't stop. I don't know how long I will have.

On the night of January 4th, a group of us had been to a preview. We drifted back to Charley Ives' place for the necessary chewing over of our impressions. I suppose there were ten people, Charley, Cora, me and a beau of mine who doesn't matter, and others. Kent Shaw was among those present. I don't know how he inserted himself but we were all used to Kent's turning up and tagging along. What seemed more important, Mildred Garrick was there.

Cora sat in one of Charley's big fat chairs. Half past midnight, which brought us, in New York, to January 5th, she put aside her glass. I saw her give a little sigh. Mildred, who had been pumping me for my opinion of the play we'd seen, soon nudged me. "There she goes! Look! Look at Steffani!"

Charley was already bending over her.

"Wait a minute," cried Mildred. "Let her alone, everybody. Who's got the correct time? Ah, there, Kent darling, I suppose you just happened to bring your tape recorder?"

Charley gave her a chilly glance. "There is no tape recorder here."

"No?" said Mildred mockingly. "Well, well."

Kent Shaw got all the implications, bared his teeth in a voiceless snarl, went far across the room and sat down, looking venomous.

"Who here takes shorthand?" Mildred demanded. A girl named Helen said she did. "All right." Mildred had taken over. "Now Cora is going to come out of it, and mark the time, somebody, when she does. And you, Helen, dear, take down everything she says."

"Why, Mildred?" asked Charley.

"Because," said Mildred, "if this is a stunt, it's a damned good one, is all as I can say." Mildred had a row of pink seashells mounted on a comb thrust behind her crown of braids. She wore a pink crepe evening dress and she stood belligerently, with her feet apart, the crepe clinging to some bad bulges along her hip bones. Charley turned his back on her.

He lifted one of Cora's very limp hands, very gently. I went near. Cora's head lolled on the chair. She looked completely out. She was wearing red, a dress that came up high around her throat and was topped with a necklace of jet. She wore tiny jet earrings. Her lipstick looked cracked and raw on the limp silence of her mouth. I looked down on her with nothing but bewilderment.

Charley said softly, "Don't worry, Ollie. We'll wait a little."

It lacked a few seconds of 12:40 when Cora came to herself abruptly, as before, in a ring of watching faces. This Helen sat on the floor with pencil and paper.

46

"Dreaming, dear?" said Mildred with a nasty little edge to the question.

Cora swallowed and the jet choker gleamed.

"Don't say a word if you don't want to," I said. "Maybe we should get a doctor."

But Cora paid me no attention. Her gaze went through me to the wall. "I walked into a restaurant," she said, "with dark walls, hideous oil paintings. I had on my brown broadcloth suit and my beaver collar. I seemed to be standing there alone. People at the tables. Then I saw one face I thought I knew. I walked up to his table . . ." Her face showed us a flash of fear. "I said, 'Pardon me, sir, isn't your name Mr. Monti? I know I've seen you. I'm Cora Steffani. I seem to be confused. Where is this place?' "

Cora stopped talking.

"And where was it?" snapped Mildred.

"The Boar's Head Tavern," Cora muttered.

"Where?"

"In Chicago." Her voice rose. "In *Chicago*."

"What did the man say?" asked Charley Ives calmly.

"He . . . didn't know what to make of it." Cora raised her hands as high as her shoulders. Now she looked at our faces, fearfully. "I don't either."

"What happened?"

"They wanted to help me," said Cora impatiently. "But I ran. I went through a revolving door. It was cold. And then it was over."

She began to shake.

"Who was the man?"

"His last name is Monti. He's a cellist. Plays with the Mannheimer Symphonic. I don't know the man. I know who he is. Why should I dream about him? It *wasn't* a dream." Cora's thin hands, that betray more age than her face, were clenching and twisting.

Mildred Garrick and some of the others pressed her with more questions but Cora only shook her head and would not answer. She looked on the verge of hysteria.

Charley said to me, "I'm going to get rid of these people and call Doc Harper. You stay, will you please, Ollie? I think she ought to go to bed, right here. Help me, will you?"

Of course I said I would. So Charley picked her up out of that chair and carried her back through a long hall into his bedroom and I trotted after. Charley went to block people out. I helped Cora undress and got her into Charley's huge pajamas.

I said, "Cora, if you need to talk you know you can talk to me."

"Oh, Ollie, it's gone," she said. "It goes just as a dream goes. I think there were several other people, but it fades. It's gone, now. All I sharply remember is as much as I said out loud. You know. Didn't you ever tell a dream, at breakfast? You can't tell *any more of it*, ever. Only this *isn't* dreaming. There's something wrong with me, Ollie. It's a relief when everything fades. . . ." She kept up that shaking. But when I touched her, she wasn't cold.

I got her into Charley's bed and she turned her face to the wall. When the doctor came, I left them and went back to the living room.

Mildred was still there. She turned from the phone. "Got them. A milk plane, or something."

"Got what?"

"Seats to Chicago. Charley and I are going to fly out, right quick."

"What *for?*"

"To talk to this man, of course. This Angelo Monti. He's in Chicago, tonight, all right. I've checked that."

"You don't mean you are going to all that trouble?"

"Somebody," said Mildred, putting her finger on it, "is going to a lot of trouble to fool us, if that's what it is."

"Well?" said Kent Shaw from where he still sat in the corner. "You're willing to be fooled?" His little dark face was furious.

"Sure. I'll be fooled in a good cause," said Mildred. "If this checks out like Jo Crain did, what a darling story!"

"Ollie, you'll stay here with Cora?" Charley said to me, looking as if even he might be on the verge of getting worried. "Keep her doing whatever the doctor says. Tell her where I'm going and why."

"You tell her," I said. "I don't know."

Kent Shaw said, half-screaming, "Why? Yes, why are you two fools going to bite on this bait? Spend your money? Go roaring off?"

"None of your business," said Mildred indifferently, "is it, little man?"

"I don't want any part of it. I want out! You're never going to make me believe any cheap second-rate—"

"The way out is straight ahead of you," said Charley Ives.

Kent pranced nervously the length of the room to the foyer. He looked back. Couldn't resist it. "Angels

49

and ministers of grace," he began to declaim. Then he seemed to choke and ducked away.

"You know what?" said Mildred. "I think the little fella is scared just about sick. Superstitious. Well, well."

I said lightly, "That or he's mad with jealousy because somebody *else* cooked this thing up."

Then I was sorry. I hadn't meant to say "true" or "false" about Cora Steffani. I saw Charley let his lashes down. He was going to fly off, affording the time, affording the money. He wouldn't say "true" or "false."

"Which is what Kent Shaw *would* think," I amended lamely.

I, too, would stand by.

We forgot Kent Shaw. Actually, he had just stepped off stage and that was his exit line. It took control to walk out before he knew if he'd won the second toss. But he had written it that way. Now he had played all the bit part he had written in for himself.

Dr. Harper, classmate and friend-of-old to Charley Ives, found nothing apparently wrong with Cora. He gave her a sedative on some kind of general principle. Three of them bustled off. It was after 2:00 A.M. Charley's spacious apartment, a whole floor of an old house, was silent. Cora seemed asleep in Charley's bed. I prowled the silent place. I lay on the couch in my slip with a blanket over me. I looked at the dim tall ranks of Charley's books on the walls. I, as they say, tossed.

Charley was out in the town getting checks cashed by friendly bartenders, picking up Mildred, making that plane.

50

What did I honestly think, at that time? Why, I had no doubt at all that it was a prearranged trick between Cora and someone. I couldn't see how it was done. But I didn't think it was supernatural. I thought it was a slick silly trick and she'd get her name in the papers and I didn't mind if she did. Or didn't. I wasn't losing sleep over that.

Cora was resting easy in Charley's bed, in the bedroom I'd never seen before that night. On his dresser stood a photograph, in a chaste and narrow golden frame. It was a photograph of me. And I was a little bit upset. I didn't like it.

In the case of the Chicago incident, Kent Shaw hadn't taken much of a gamble. The proprietor of the Boar's Head Tavern happened to be no Englishman, but one Gallo, boyhood chum and compatriot to Angelo Monti. If the Mannheimer Symphonic Orchestra played in Chicago on the evening of January 4th, as it had long ago contracted to do, it was certain, barring serious illness or death itself, that Monti would be at the Boar's Head after the concert. Not to have appeared there would have shattered a long sentimental tradition and broken an unwritten law with its roots in two warm hearts. Which was unthinkable. So it was very close to a sure thing.

It paid off. Angelo Monti was in his place when the curtain went up on Scene Two.

Darlene Hite got into Chicago about noon that day (she spent the intervals taking quiet and lonely "vacations" in various country places) and went to a small obscure hotel in her decorous way. When the time came, she got into costume, the suit like Cora's, did

51

her hair up in Cora's fashion, put on another long loose garment, this time a coat with a hood. It was cold in Chicago.

She walked into the restaurant at the appointed time, with the coat over her arm, and she said her lines. Angelo Monti struggled to extricate himself from his position among his friends at the center of the banquette. His kind heart was, at once, anxious to help the strange lady, if he could. But the lady fled.

There came into the show at this moment, however, an extra scene, a bit added by that old reviser of all the best-written scripts of men.

From another table, as Darlene fled, a strange man rose up. He came swiftly over to Monti, who stood, napkin caught on his paunch, staring after the woman in brown. This stranger was tall, blond and baldish, with a florid complexion. He asked if the lady was in trouble and what her name was.

Monti said helplessly, "I don't know her."

The stranger said, "Maybe I do." So he threw money on his own table and he hurried through the revolving door.

He caught her in the act of slipping into the coat and pulling up the hood. So he touched her arm. "Darlene! Say, what do you know! Doncha remember me? Ed Jones from good old San Diego," and brayed in the cold street, "Sa-ay, long time no see!"

Darlene had to recognize him because she had to move away from this spot without argument or delay. He wanted to know if there had been any trouble. She told him she'd made a mistake of identity. She made up a reason for being in Chicago. Darlene was competent and quick. She amiably made a date with him for the following day and let him take her "home" to the wrong hotel. Through it, she walked to another exit.

But Ed Jones was unlucky. It occurred to him that he must change the hour they had set for the morrow. He went in and discovered that she was not registered and someone had seen her walk through. So Ed Jones went to that side exit and while he stood, fuming, the cab returned. By sheer bad luck, Ed Jones found out where she had gone. In the morning, when Darlene checked out and started for her bus, Ed Jones fell in beside her.

He was a stubborn and an unlucky man. A part for him had to be improvised.

On the morning of the 5th I put on my beige-and-gold theatre dress again. Cora was awake, looking lazy and well. I thought her fit of nerves, faked or not, was over. I told her I had classes and she let me go without protest. So I hurried uptown to change to sober clothing and go to work.

Ten o'clock that evening, Charley called. "We got the dope. Cora's still here. Come on down."

I'd been waiting, waiting for this call. Yet now that it had come, I didn't want to be disturbed. "Tell me on the phone, Charley, my boy," I said. "I'm tired."

Mildred had taken along a stenographer and they had Monti's remarks on paper. He didn't have the ear for lines that Jo Crain had. The correspondence was not perfect. But the time checked, the description checked, the nose had been noticed, Cora's photograph had been accepted. The bit about the strange

53

man was, of course, extra. Monti said the mysterious stranger had never returned to the restaurant.

"I suppose she vanished," I said, "and it upset him."

"Ollie, Cora's pretty upset. She—"

"Charley, I think I'd better not."

Cora had grabbed the phone. "Ollie, what can I *do?* Ollie, stay by me? Everybody is going to think I'm a freak! Please, Ollie, don't *you* leave me!" I could hear she'd been crying.

Charley took the phone. "Coming down?"

"Do you really need me? Isn't Mildred there? What can *I* do? I work, you know."

"I'm going to take Cora home," Charley said briskly. "She can't stay here."

Why not? I thought.

"She wants you to stay at her place."

"Stay? Move in, you mean?"

"She wants you, Ollie. Rather have you than anyone. Says you're her oldest friend. She shouldn't stay alone."

"Oh me," I sighed. "Oh my . . ."

"You won't do it?"

"Of course, I'll do it," I said with foreboding. "But no point in coming there where you are. I'll go directly to Cora's."

"Thanks, Teacher," said Charley. "I'll be just as glad there's some responsible—"

"Glad to oblige, Charley, my boy," said I heartily and he hung up suddenly. But I had the foreboding. I couldn't do this, and teach, too.

When I got to Cora's there was more uproar.

54

Mildred Garrick had left Charley at the airport at 9:00, treacherously saying nothing about her immediate plans. She had gone directly to Cora's apartment, bribed the maid, and searched the place. The only thing of any significance she had found was the tape. She'd made off with it.

I said it was plain burglary, which, after all, is a crime. But Cora only wrung her hands and said she couldn't fuss. That would only make it worse.

So, on January 6th, Mildred ran a whole column about Cora and her dreams of being elsewhere and the strange "fact" that people did indeed see her elsewhere, although she was here. Mildred invented the phrase, *The Dream Walker*.

Well, Josephine Crain was fit to be tied. Angelo Monti was also annoyed. *They* were above suspicion. Their annoyance and reluctance rang very true. It helped a lot.

The story was not exactly believed, of course. It was discussed. People got into arguments over such things as the relation between a supernatural manifestation and a time zone. These, however, were people in show business, a flamboyant few. Not the general public.

Yet Ned Dancer, no theatrical gossip columnist, he, was quietly asking some searching questions.

From this time forth (although we didn't know it) Cora was carefully watched. Mildred had permanently bribed the maid to look at her mail and listen to her conversations. Ned Dancer had bribed the switchboard operator, downstairs, to listen in on her phone calls. But nothing suspicious came in the mail or turned up in her conversations or transpired on the telephone. Kent Shaw was smart when he cut off communication.

Now he had dropped out; he'd washed his hands of the whole thing. He didn't come around any more.

"If this is a stunt," Mildred said to me, "it's a dilly, is all as I can say."

Cora wasn't ill, of course, and if her nerves twitched she bore up well. With callers who wanted to be told all about this business, Cora was terse, tense, and subdued. With me alone, she didn't discuss it at all. We were a pair of old acquaintances who had our secrets and were, at once, a little hostile and a little relaxed together.

On January 9th, she rehearsed and performed in a radio drama, going about her business as usual. So I went home. Cora didn't need her hand held. Or, if she did, Charley Ives was underfoot enough, hanging around, big and rather taciturn, watching us both, and suffering Cora to tease and command him. I pleaded my job. I was glad to get away.

But I was disconcerted when my girls began to ask me questions. "Miss Hudson," one said, "if *you* tell us all those statements are accurate, we'll have to believe them."

"They are accurate, as far as they go," I said, "but of course there is a great deal that's unknown."

"Miss Reynolds says it's a publicity gag."

"It may be," I said and kept smiling.

"And that it's cheap and dishonest."

They waited for my judgment to be pronounced. I said, "A publicity stunt may get an actress noticed. It

56

can't make her a better actress. Only work can do that." (Always the teacher.)

"Cora Steffani must be pretty good," one said didactically, "or else *you* would see she was faking. Maybe you do, Miss Hudson."

Those kids can really get you into a corner. "I don't easily accept the supernatural," I said. "Let's leave it at that."

But then, of course, one brought up extra-sensory perception. And another spoke solemnly of one's duty to keep an open mind.

I had to say that we weren't there to decide between such alternatives and could not, without more knowledge. I reminded them that what you kept your mind open *for* was not idle amazement, but more knowledge. "Don't open your minds so wide that they hold nothing," I told them severely. "And don't be sheep, either."

"We aren't sheep," one said.

"Then why is every girl in this room wearing her hair short and brushed upward all around her head?"

"Because *you* do, Miss Hudson," one said sheepishly.

"Then I'm a poor teacher," I said.

Next day their heads were riotously different, each from the others. Oh, I suppose it's a backwater, it's unimportant, this work of mine. I did enjoy them, my innocent imps, my frivolous angels, my worried ones, my sly ones, and the few with shining eyes.

CHAPTER 5

The 15th of January was Marcus' birthday. We flew down that morning. I wouldn't let Charley Ives call for me but it seemed perverse of him to make the airport at the last minute. As we went aboard, bearing gifts, Charley said if he'd thought of it he'd have brought me an orchid.

"You are thoughtful," I said, "but since I think an orchid is a floozy, it's just as well."

He said that, off-hand, he couldn't think of an intel-lectual-type flower. Could I? I flounced onto that plane. I had plenty of physical room in my seat, next the window, but Charley *filled* that plane, of course. I felt barricaded by his body from all the near world and on my other side the world fell far. I watched the city go by under and then there was New Jersey. "I'm going to doze," I said firmly and wedged the little pil-low under my neck.

"Cousin Ollie," said Charley. I was wide awake. "A question will have to be asked. I don't want to fight, mind you. But what do I *do,* that you haven't any pa-tience with me?"

I said, "Nothing." A look of long-suffering came

upon his face. "I mean that," I said indignantly. "What do you do for a living?"

"For a living?" he drawled. "Why, nothing much."

"So I've seen," said I. My heart was pounding. I didn't want to fight.

"Where did *you* get this Puritan idea?" asked Charley after about a hundred miles of earth had turned and put itself behind us.

"I'm no Puritan."

"About work. Work, for the night is coming."

I got it from *you,* I thought, outraged. But I said wearily, "I suppose I've found out there's no other way to be even moderately happy."

Charley said, after pondering, "You may be right, Teacher." Then he grinned down, the maddening way he does. "You mean to say, whenever I got up the nerve to ask you this, you'd have answered?"

"Let's not have questions and answers, please. Teacher's tired."

"Doze," he said. "Doze, by all means."

I couldn't even shut my eyes.

"If *you* made a promise," Charley said to the plane's ceiling, "*you* wouldn't break it."

"Not if I could help it."

"Hard work and high principles," he muttered. "All this and Art, too."

Now I shut my eyes tight because they were stinging with the start of tears. "You make me sound like a prig," I said. "All right. Maybe I am."

"There are those who would say so," said Charley Ives, and I had a distinct vision of Cora Steffani's mocking face.

"Have you promised to marry Cora again?" I said loudly, to my dismay.

"Uh uh," said Charley. His eyes flashed blue.

"Why not?" I cried, idiotically.

"Now, really," drawled Charley with an eyebrow cocked.

"Sorry," I said, looking out at New Jersey or whatever it was. "Just vulgar human curiosity."

Charley was as quiet as a mouse. After a while he stirred in the seat. "You've got everything hindside forward," he began. "You always had."

"Charley," I said in something like panic. "Truly, I can't be your confidante."

In a moment he asked, "Why? Are you Cora's? Just in a spirit of vulgar human curiosity, has Cora told you this trance business is a fake?"

"No. She has not." I was all prepared to be a little bit hurt.

"Nor me either," said Charley. "But, Ollie, you *know* it's got to be."

I looked at him and sighed. We both smiled. "She'd do it," he said, "just for the hell of it."

"I know. But how can she be working it?"

"Beats me."

"She'd have to have a double," said I. "They could have figured that Jo Crain would be on that beach. But I can't understand that Chicago business." (We didn't know about Mr. Gallo at this point.) "How could they figure out that one?"

"Couldn't," said Charley, "without signals. What signal is instantaneous over a thousand miles?"

"The common ordinary household telephone, for one."

"True. True. But there was no phone call. Was there?"

"Not that I know."

"She may go on with it and pull another one."

"No telling when or where, either," I said.

"Well, I suppose the sky's not going to fall if Cora gets a little newspaper space."

"It isn't hurting anyone," I agreed, just as ignorantly.

"Interesting character, my ex," said Charley lazily.

"Of course," I said.

"Do you like rascals, Ollie?"

"Some."

"Energetic ones, eh?"

I looked out the window.

"I expect *you* wouldn't hurt anyone," Charley said after a while. "Scruples, you'd have." I stiffened. "But don't you ever get tangled up among your principles?" he teased me. "Loyally, you come when Cora calls. Although you're pretty sure she is a fraud."

I started to say, I came when *you* called. "We've known each other a million years," I said, instead. "Once, we were young—"

"Poor . . . old . . . thing," said Charley softly.

"Charley, my boy," I said, "will you please not needle me all the way to Washington? I knew I shouldn't have got on this plane with you."

"I'm just a grasshopper, trying to get along with an ant," said Charley cheerfully. "Though it seems to me, once it was the other way around."

"It *never*," I began indignantly. Then he kissed me. "What—!" I sputtered.

"Go to sleep," said Charley Ives. "Improve the shining hour." He settled back, looking pleased with himself.

I rode the rest of the way with my eyes closed but my mind was frantically trying to figure out what promise he had made to whom, and if not to Cora, then why did he let her act as if she owned him? Isn't it a strange thing that you can get to be thirty-four years old and presumably mature, and still catch your mind carrying on as if it were in high school? I was *consumed* with vulgar curiosity. I *couldn't* ask.

When we got to Marcus' big, gracious, and delightfully shabby house, the clan had gathered, sure enough. Charley promptly disappeared. Since he fills a room, the big lug, by the same token when he isn't there he leaves an awful space. He didn't turn up again until dinner time and he didn't explain. Marcus seemed to know where he had been. But then Marcus seems, sometimes, to know everything.

God bless him, dear Marcus. He's not a large person physically. He is rather slight and rather small. Whatever his features were when he was young, handsome or otherwise, by now, in the years of his life, he has carved his own face. And it is beautiful. I suppose that's true. Every thought and every feeling that seems to run through the brain and the body so swiftly and briefly, still leaves the mark of its passing. Just as water drops that have long reached and disappeared in the sea, each and all made the river-bed through which they came. It's a terrible true thing.

It did you good to look at Marcus. His face was his biography.

He was pleased with the gaudy brace of thrillers I'd brought. He said only Charley catered to his sneaking passion for blood and detection. "Charley!" I was surprised. "Tries to keep me supplied," Marcus said, "but it's peanut reading. You can't stop till they're all gone."

Marcus isn't grim. He's easy. He's tucked into life as if he enjoys it, just as it is. So, while Marcus can talk to you about any subject at all, still, when you are with him—I don't know—the wind blows wider.

The puzzling business of a woman who seemed to be able to be two places at once fell out of my consciousness until Charley Ives, after dinner, chose to tell about it. The company (oh, there was Charley's mother, Virginia Ives, and his sister, Joanna, and Sally Davies, Charley's first cousin, and her husband, Sig Rudolf, and my parents, Millicent and George, and Charley's brother, J.P.; and there was the help, Johnny Cunneen, Marcus' secretary, and the little sub-secretary, Ruthie Miller, and his stately housekeeper, Mrs. Doone) *all* of them, it seemed to me, began to argue.

Those who scoffed and wanted to dismiss an unimportant bit of nonsense met a stern demand for a reasonable explanation. Whoever tentatively got wistful about ghosts ran into hard-headed laughter. That was the way it worked, of course.

Marcus himself said little. He did say that if it was a trick, it must have been planned for a long time and it must cost something (money and brains). "Is publicity of that kind worth so much, Ollie?"

"I can't see that it is, Uncle John."

(But of course Marcus sees clearly. Money, brains, *and a purpose*. Yet nobody, not even he, could have guessed, in January, what the purpose was.)

Sally and Sig Rudolf flew back with us and she bent my ear all the way with what she calls problems. They dropped me at my apartment. Marcus was safely seventy-six, and it had been a good day.

I suspect I ramble. The plot. The plotters.

I suppose Raymond Pankerman, seeing Mildred's column, was gratified as the plot sprang to life. Cora was probably hugging himself with wicked joy. Kent Shaw, however, must have been devastated by anxiety.

Who was the stranger who thought he recognized Darlene? And had he recognized Darlene? Or *Cora? It made a difference.* If he recognized Cora (and Darlene got away) well and good. But, in either case, if Darlene *hadn't* got away, then there was someone who had seen too clearly into the hocus pocus backstage. Kent Shaw, that dark, bitter, driving little man, exiled by his own cold cleverness from the middle of the excitement, hard-headedly keeping away—how he must have suffered! For Darlene, who could have communicated (since they had a device arranged for an emergency) did not.

Darlene, in fact, was having a difficult time. This Edward Jones had conceived the perfectly sound idea that Darlene had tried to brush him off. But, stubborn and perverse as he was, hard-to-get meant had-to-get to him. And Darlene knew, even better than Kent Shaw knew yet, that Ed Jones certainly could blow up the machinery of the trick any time he chose. So she knew it had been a mistake—it wouldn't be smart at all to brush him off.

She let him follow her to the ranch in Texas where she was taking another of those "vacations." In fact, she teased him and tried to keep him near. She was worried. It was all right, so far, because he hadn't seen Mildred's column, not being interested in her kind of gossip, and no discussing was being done in Texas. Yet. But Darlene knew that if all went as planned, there would soon be pictures, pictures of Cora Steffani. What could prevent Ed Jones from popping up to say not only that he knew the same nose on another woman's face, but that he knew it *was* the other woman, Darlene Hite, who had been in a tavern in Chicago, *saying she was Cora Steffani*.

Darlene finally made a decision on her own. She was forced to do so. The third incident nearly ran them into disaster.

CHAPTER 6

nt Shaw was really clever. I had already heard
e people say that it seemed significant, how Cora
amed in a crowd. "Makes sure she has an audience,
esn't she?" some said.

So when she dreamed and walked in the dream for
e third time, she dreamed in quite different circum-
tances.

This was not solely for variety's sake. This time it
was a wild throw. The risk of failure was great. Even
with success, the timing could not be exact. It had to
be left somewhat vague so that there would be a safe
margin. Therefore, this time no tape recorder and no
shorthand could be allowed and no witness, either,
who would have any idea what was supposed to be
happening. The two witnesses were unimpeachable,
just the same. A cabdriver drawn from the traffic's
grab bag, and a cop who happened to be by.

Two solid citizens, then, who thought they had a
fainting woman on their hands. Who exchanged
glances when Cora sat up suddenly in the cab, early in
the afternoon of February 10th, took paper from her
purse and began to scribble on it.

The driver had gone to the curb and hailed the cop.

The cop had opened the cab's door. *They* wanted name, address, and diagnosis. Scribbling, they couldn't wait for.

"Lady," the cop said, "if you're okay, the driver will take you home. If you want a doctor . . . Lady . . . Listen, Ma'am . . ."

"Don't speak," cried Cora, scribbling.

"Don't get mad," the driver said. "You was out. So what was it? A fit or something? Hey, lady!"

Cora, of course, stopped her scribbling exactly when she chose to stop. The cab took her home. She called me. The maid heard her and called Mildred Garrick. The operator downstairs called Ned Dancer. I called Charley Ives because Cora asked me to.

So there we were.

Cora was still huddled in her camel's hair topcoat. "Happened again and it's gone," she told us. "It's lost. I tried to write it all down but they were so impatient. Maybe it doesn't matter. Maybe it's just as well. Only I'd rather know." She seemed to be in a state. While Charley comforted her, I took the piece of paper. She'd scribbled on the back of an old script and the writing was big and agitated.

"Snow," I read. "Everything white. Cold. Galoshes. Blue ski suit. Mittens and cap. Wild country. Empty. Man on the path. Bundled up. Dark clothes. White hair. Long, long jaw. Gray eyes. Said, 'Is there anything at all I can do for you?' Irish. I said, 'I'm lost. When did it snow? Which way is New York?' He pointed. I ran. Slipping in snow. Trees. A mountain. Voice calling after me . . ."

"That's all there is," I said. I sorted out those

67

disjointed words and made a scene of them in my mind.

"What did the voice call?" Charley wanted to know. I thought his question was an odd choice out of all the possible questions.

Cora just shook her head and wailed. "I've told you and told you how it fades."

"Where did this happen?" asked Mildred.

"I took a cab down from NBC. I must have passed out. I don't know where."

"When?" Ned Dancer demanded.

"Don't know when, either. I suppose you could find the driver. But I can't tell how long I'd been out before he noticed. I came to and there was a policeman. You could ask."

"Don't think we won't," Ned Dancer said.

"I meant," said Mildred, "where's all this snow and stuff? Where did you think you were?"

"I'd been there before," said Cora in a low voice. "I think it was Aspen. Aspen, Colorado."

Charley got up jerkily and began to walk around.

"Come now," said Mildred gently.

"*Don't* believe it!" Cora cried. "*Prove* to me it isn't so! I *want* you to! Please!"

Ned Dancer went to the telephone. Charley said slowly, "We can fly out . . ."

Ned said, "I intend to."

Charley said, "To prove anything, Cora, you'll have to go, too." She looked terrified.

"That's quite right," I said. "You can't go to bed and hide your head. That is, if you want to prove anything. The man with the long jaw, if you can find him, will have to see you face to face. And so will Josephine Crain. And so will Angelo Monti."

Cora made moaning sounds. "Ollie, can you come?" she whimpered.

"Ollie has work to do," said Charley Ives quickly.

"That's true. I couldn't possibly go," said I.

Cora looked up at Ned Dancer who is a slim smooth-faced man with the coldest eye in the world. "Do I have to go? Mildred, are you going?"

Mildred stood there, sucking a tooth. She had on a gray suit and a sharp black feather stuck at a jaunty angle in her hair. Mildred's eyes were cold, too, and shrewd.

"No use for me to go to the mountain," she said phlegmatically. "Neddy, here, is going to have it on the front page before I could use it. I'll have to sob about it, later. Cheer up, dear," she said to Cora. "Charley will protect you. And how can you lose? If you weren't walking in Colorado, why then you'll feel better, won't you? If you were, you'll only be slightly notorious."

Cora was crying and carrying on and clinging to Charley. Dancer was on the phone. Mildred slipped out to speak quietly with the maid in the kitchenette.

I sat with that piece of paper in my hand. For the first time, I was frightened. It seemed *too much,* somehow. Too elaborate. I suppose my mind was following the hint from Marcus. Expensive. Who could pay? Not Cora. She was always a lap behind her bills. (Certainly not Kent Shaw. Everyone knew how poor he was.) If it was a trick—*someone* was paying. And how was all this to be worth what it cost? What could be its purpose?

They flew to Colorado. Charley Ives, Cora Steffani and Ned Dancer. I taught my classes.

Charley told me, when they got back, that the first thing the Reverend Thomas Barron, clergyman, of Denver, said to them in his Irish lilt was this sentence, "Is there anything at all I can do for you?" Of course the dear man said it a thousand times a week. He had said it to Darlene Hite. Cora, in New York, had *quoted* him. You can see the power in that.

Charley said to me, "Coz, do you realize that, up until now, there was no direct quotation from the other side? What Cora said, yes. But Cora never quote directly a word Jo Crain said, or this Monti, either."

"I hadn't realized," I admitted. "But of course, you are right."

"This man in Colorado says it to everyone," Charley explained. "What gets me is how could Cora Steffani *know* that?"

"I don't see how she could know it," I said gravely. "She must be frightened."

Charley looked down at me with a sharp turn of his head. But I was shriveled in the cab's corner. We were on our way to hear the tape recording that Ned Dancer had made in Colorado.

The thing was, I'd been tossing, while Cora and Charley were away. One night I sat up in my bed. I'd been *seeing* Cora tucked in against a plane's window and Charley's big body barricading all the world away. I sat up and had a session with myself in the dark. None of *that*, Olivia, I said to myself. Don't be a snob, of all things. Cora was in the family once already, and if she is going to be in it again, remember

70

it's not up to you to wince. What's the matter with you? You're practically living vicariously. Tend to yourself. Live as *you* must. Be what *you* ought. So I had got myself in hand.

"Ollie, *you're* not beginning to think she walks in some astral body?" Charley looked incredulous.

"No. But I don't *know* what's going on," I said, "and I've decided that until I do *know* more, I'm going to stand by. We've known each other a long time. Most people are going to draw away from her. I won't be one of them, yet. I don't think I want to talk behind her back, either." I didn't add that I thought it was outrageous that he did. I tried not to think it. That was his business.

"Okay, Teacher," said Charley in a stunned way. And then we were there, at Ned's office.

Cora wasn't along. (Neither was Kent Shaw and nobody gave him a thought.) Yet Ned played the interview back for quite a group of us that evening. The affair was getting less and less private.

"Dr. Barron," Ned began on the tape, respectfully, "since we want to get this on record, today is the 11th of February, is it not?"

"It is." (The moment I heard those two syllables in that rich voice I knew that *here* was a witness farther above suspicion than the Rockies are above the plains.)

"You are the Reverend Thomas Barron of Denver. We are now in Aspen."

"I am and we are. Go ahead, lad."

"Now, yesterday, you were out for a walk, sir?"

"I was."

Charley's voice came in. "Pardon me. You go for

71

these solitary walks pretty often? As a regular thing?"

"I do. I come here, see, for the two weeks every winter. I'm not spry enough for the sports, long is the day, but I can still walk, praise God. So I do a good bit of walking alone and looking about and breathing the good air. Then, by night, I'm jolly with the younger ones around the fire. It all does me good, I believe, both the one and the other."

"Yes, sir." Even Ned's cold voice was softened. "Now, you met this lady yesterday on the path. Had you ever seen her before?"

"I had not. What is it," Dr. Barron said blithely, "the amnesia? Now, my dear, don't you worry. It's a prevalent thing, that, it seems to me, but no one the worse for it that I ever heard of. What is it you want me to say now?"

"Just tell us what happened, sir," Ned said resignedly.

Charley prodded. "And the time."

"The time? Now, I was heading *to* the Lodge, so it would be near my noon meal. I can't say closer. I was a mile off and coming up. This young lady was coming down. I don't know if she stopped me or if it was only the look of her that stopped me. I had not seen her before in my life. I said to her, 'Is there anything at all I can do for you?' I said."

Gasps came into the recorded sounds.

"What is it? Eh?" No one answered so the minister went on. "And she said to me that she was lost. I think she also spoke of the snow. Then she wanted me to say where New York was lying. Before I could get my wits together—"

72

"Did you point, sir?"

"I may have pointed but I doubt it. I haven't the head for geography. But she didn't stay, see. She ran away then."

"Did you shout after her?"

"I don't remember that I did and I don't remember that I didn't. I did wish she had stayed so that I could find out what was the matter."

"You didn't follow, sir?"

"I'm not so fit for haring after a young woman in the snow, which is a pity. All I could do, I watched, and her running down that path. Then the man leapt from a bush."

"What man!"

"How should I know what man? A big man, it was, although too far for to see clear. He took her roughly with his hands and I didn't like the look of *that* and I would have gone down. But he stopped it and they slipped their arms around each other's backs, do you see, and off they went. And it was a friend, my dear, and you're all right now?"

"You didn't mention a second man, Cora?" Ned's accusing voice.

"I know," Cora's was a terrified croak. "I can't remember . . . now now . . ."

"Now whatever it is," Dr. Barron said chidingly, "you mustn't be pestering her."

"You will swear that this is the young lady you met on the path yesterday?"

"I don't know that I'll swear at all," the minister said.

"But you—"

Charley's voice interrupted. "Can you tell us what she was wearing?"

"Why, the very clothing she is now. The blue trousers and all. But she'd a scarlet cap on her head and very becoming, too."

"It's at home," Cora's croak.

"Now, I've said all I'm going to say." Dr. Barron's charming voice was stern again. "This young lady is in some trouble and it's scaring the voice into her throat and you'll tell me the trouble and we'll do what we can."

"We are all her friends, sir," Ned Dancer said tensely. "If you can swear, one way or the other, it will put her mind at rest. Is this the same young lady?"

"Maybe it is and maybe it isn't," Dr. Barron said, "but it's plain to me she's more upset today than she was yesterday, and until you'll tell me what's the matter, I'll do no swearing and that thing listening."

That was the end of the tape.

I asked them what Dr. Barron had thought of Cora's side of the story. Charley smiled. "The old gentleman didn't turn a hair. Said the Lord would make it all clear if and when He felt like it, and in the meantime, people should not pester each other." I had to smile, too.

"But did he swear it was Cora?" demanded Mildred.

"No, he never did swear."

"This second man," I mused, "surely he should turn up once he sees the papers."

Mildred Garrick said sourly the second man was no doubt Cora's demon lover.

74

He didn't turn up.

The story was in the papers, all right, but it was, at first, treated gingerly and briefly. The news magazines picked it up for an oddity. Then came Mildred's column, making the most of it. Sobbing, as she'd promised. *Dream Walker in the snow!* Finally, Ned Dancer plastered it, complete, over two pages of a Sunday supplement, with dialogue and pictures. The captions were impressive. "First lady of the American theatre, Josephine Crain." "Well-known musician, Angelo Monti." "Beloved Clergyman, Thomas Barron." "New York Publisher, Charles Marcus Ives." And even, "Olivia Hudson, 34, teacher in fashionable girls' school." Oh, plenty of class this story had!

And Cora Steffani couldn't have swallowed a gnat, without it being known, so closely was she watched after that.

I went down to stay with her again because she said she was afraid to be alone. Charley Ives wanted to hire a nurse, or the like. I said she needed a friend. He said impatiently that he was her friend as much as I was and he'd see she was taken care of. I said she'd asked for me. He said, "You don't want to get mixed up in it." I said whether I wanted to or not, I seemed to *be* mixed up in it. We almost fought.

But I had to go.

Oh, I should have known, if I hadn't been so busy with *my* conscience, that Cora asked for me, and mixed me up in it, and wanted to use my unimpeachable testimony to hurt a dear old gentleman I adored, for much the same reason I had to let her do it.

75

CHAPTER 7

It was February. The plot was working up splendidly.

Was it?

The trouble was, Darlene Hite had to tell Ed Jones. She had hoped to slip away from him to do the Colorado bit. She knew something would have to be done about him, but she was caught by the appointed day, and she thought she could get back to the Texas place before anything broke. But he followed her. He was suspicious and had nothing to do but indulge his suspicions, and he was in a mean mood. Been teased, I suppose, more than he could bear. Although he was a mean person, I should think. So there was that scene in the snow. And she told him.

She said, "Don't, Ed. It's only my job. I'll tell you all about it." And she slipped her arm around his back (as Dr. Barron said). "I'm not supposed to tell a soul," she said, "but I'll tell *you*."

She told him it was a publicity stunt because that's what she thought it was.

Ed Jones knew at once that he was in a position to spoil the fun. Darlene knew he knew and faced up to this as one does in the jungle. She gave him money.

She said her boss would realize what a good idea this was. She said if Ed would be quiet she'd speak to her boss and see if she could get him a job, too.

Ed Jones had a little money, not enough, of course. He was a drifting person, not steadily employed. He thought he'd stumbled into an easy job, "helping" Darlene. He must have known perfectly well that it was blackmail of a kind. He rather liked being backstage. He was interested in money, but he wasn't reliably devoted to money and Darlene knew this. She had to manage as best she could.

The two of them started for San Francisco in his car. The whole scheme now rode on whether Ed Jones would stay sober or be able to bear reading the papers without boasting that he knew a thing or two. Darlene managed him, somehow.

Now, possibly Raymond Pankerman was pleased at what he read and heard, and thought it was going well. Maybe he sat among his lawyers, fighting his paper battles, and out of the side of his eye he watched his chance of revenge, as it grew. And maybe Cora simmered inside with mirth and excitement. But Kent Shaw must have been frantic!

What *about* that man in Chicago? Who *was* that second man in the snow? Kent Shaw was the writer-director-producer. Not to know must have driven him wild!

On the 5th of March, Darlene Hite called, at a prearranged hour, the assigned number of the phone in the booth of the mediocre little bar where Kent took care to be every third evening. When he stepped into the booth, nodded to the barman that this call was his,

77

he must have thanked whatever gods he had, to hear her voice.

Darlene told him the San Francisco incident was out. George Jocelyn, the writer, had taken off unexpectedly on a trip. What they had planned with him couldn't be done. Kent Shaw would tip Cora? . . . Yes, yes, but what about this *man*? . . . So Darlene told him all about Ed Jones.

"*Told* him!" Kent shrieked. And pressing for an end that Darlene didn't even know about, the ruin of John Paul Marcus, he must have rummaged for and found the inspiration. How he could save his beautiful scheme, that was going so beautifully well. How he could not only save it but improve it. And gamble everything. All in the world Kent Shaw had left to put on the table.

So he said, "Give him more money. As much as you have to. Tell him, if he opens his mouth, there will be no more money. For you or for him. Keep him close to you and quiet. Skip San Francisco. But meet me in Los Angeles earlier. March 25th." He told her where. "I'll have a job for him. In the meantime, lie low somewhere. Fly to Honolulu. It's a quick flight from where you are. You can have a nice time in the islands. No matter what you do, keep him quiet and tell him nothing *more*. I'll see you myself in L.A. The 25th of March."

So Kent Shaw hung up and now the brain had to gather the wavering shadow of his solution and bring it out of nothing into solid plan. He had to incorporate Ed Jones usefully into the plot. He did it brilliantly, I suppose. Certainly, the one thing Kent Shaw could not bear was to see his work spoiled, now. Now, that the plot was rolling, it had gone this far with such success. Impossible for Kent Shaw to accept exposure and defeat, now, in the glow of achievement. For an Ed Jones? A man who had happened to be in a tavern in Chicago? A character rung into the cast by that bad playwright, coincidence?

It was too bad. But perhaps it was not necessarily bad, at all. Perhaps it was good. Perhaps it supplied a missing element of strength, of depth. Why yes, it did. It could.

Kent Shaw saw ahead. But I wonder how far.

Los Angeles is murky. It is still murky. But first I can tell you how Cora and Kent Shaw had a conference. Kent Shaw managed this by, outrageously, breaking a taboo.

I was living with Cora through February and into March. I went back and forth to my school. But she gave up working almost entirely. So far, the affair had not helped her employability. Perhaps because those who employed her saw, as yet, no fierce public curiosity. The strong interest, the lively talk, was still more or less within the trade. Therefore, there were too many interruptions, in the studios, and too much time lost, because of the curious who wanted to speak to her or anyhow look at her. The role she played lasted twenty-four hours a day. Every evening people came in.

Sometimes I think the ones who would not talk kept the talk alive. Josephine Crain refused to see Cora and to speak of it at all. Even Angelo Monti's good nature

79

had its limits. He saw Cora and rather reluctantly identified her and thereafter would not discuss it. Dr. Barron became, I understand, sweetly adamant and not a word would he say. I didn't talk, Lord knows. And Cora found a mask-like look, very sweet and sad and meek, a pawn-of-fate look that she put on. She wouldn't talk very much. Just enough.

Charley Ives would turn up some evenings and sit there in Cora's big room for an hour or two, keeping his eye on her. Oh, Cora was watched from all sides. *I* watched her. So there was argument and speculation and baffled curiosity around the town, but nobody watching saw anything.

February went into March and March went along. Nobody noticed that Cora went to a certain tea-roomish eating place not a block from her apartment in a kind of pattern. She'd go Monday and Thursday. The next week, Tuesday and Friday. The following week, Wednesday and Saturday. This had been going on since December and the pattern was inconspicuous. The place was convenient and a habit. Yet, if Kent Shaw were to come in while she was there, and if he made any occasion to tuck his napkin into his collar, it was a signal. It meant that the next planned incident must be discarded.

On March 8th, Cora and I were in this place, having a bachelor-girl kind of evening meal. When Kent Shaw came in, I saluted him, and Cora nodded, but he simply glowered. He didn't come over to speak to us. I thought he was still either superstitious or envious and didn't bother to decide which. Kent Shaw seemed to me to be the same shabby relic of himself he'd been for years. Oh, I saw him put the napkin up and tuck it around his collar and pick up the supremely dry and unjuicy bit of fried chicken in his fingers. I didn't wonder. It meant nothing to me.

"Kent's an odd one," I said to Cora. "I'd have thought he'd have been right in the thick of all this dream life of yours, spouting theories. You?"

Cora shrugged. "Sorry little man. Burnt himself out, years ago."

"Speaking of getting burnt, are you giving up?" I asked her.

"Giving up what?" She peered over her glasses.

"Theatre?"

"Never."

"I don't notice you running around to see who's casting."

"Ollie, I can't. You know that. I mean, not now."

"For how long can't you?"

She pulled her glasses down to hang around her neck and looked at me thoughtfully. "Oh, this will die down," she said lamely. "I may never have a dream again."

"If you do, I advise you to see some doctors," I said. (I don't know why.)

Cora took hold of her glass of water and her fingers whitened. "At least you can see it's an affliction," she said angrily. "Most people think it's a great joke. I've got a notion to go ahead and get married again and the hell with it."

I was startled. I know my mouth opened. Then, I knew that although she stared at her plate which was probably a blur to her without her reading glasses, she

81

was really, by nerve and ear and eye corner, watching me. I felt a wind of malice.

"You think if you get married again you'll stop this dreaming?" I asked her in my most detached manner.

"They do say it's the end of dreaming," she murmured facetiously.

I could have asked her if she'd found it so. She'd never talked to me about Charley Ives, nor told me why she had so soon divorced him. But I didn't ask. I never had.

Kent Shaw got up, then abruptly sat down again, studied his check. A signal. Cora's head turned slowly. "Why haven't you ever married, Ollie?" she cooed.

"I'd rather dream," said I.

"Of course, you do have your work," Cora grinned nastily. "I suppose the high-brow temple of Fine Art where you serve couldn't do without you."

Kent Shaw was now arguing with the cashier. He paid, with an air of anger, and he left the place.

"It better not do without me tonight. I've got some grades to figure." I could always pretend her cracks didn't hit me. "So shall we . . . ?"

"In a minute," said Cora, swigging coffee. "No offense, huh, Teacher? Excuse me, Ollie?"

She went to the "Ladies." And I sat, wondering whether I was fond of her or not. Whether she hadn't become more like a relative with whom I was involuntarily entangled. Whether she would soon become a relative (in law) again.

Meanwhile, Kent Shaw nipped around the corner, went in a side passage, and broke a taboo. He rapped on the "Ladies" and Cora let him in. The door was in nobody's view, back in a warren of interior partitions. I didn't suspect a thing. I'd seen Kent Shaw go out of the building. I didn't even know there was that other way in. When Cora came back, we paid and walked home. Me to my work, to sit remembering my girls and assessing their progress and being too generous, I suspect. (And beating down that question. *Who* wanted Cora to marry him, again, and had been refused, so far? And *how* had I gotten it hindside forward?)

Meanwhile, Cora sat before the TV set, swinging one ankle, smoking, looking lazy, but inside the dark head, the brain was busy memorizing new instructions.

Kent Shaw told her there would be no San Francisco episode because Jocelyn, the writer, had gone away. Therefore, he thought it wise to move the Los Angeles episode ahead in time. Iron was hot, best to strike, and all that. But he said he was leery about Patrick Davenport's eye. Davenport, that famous movie director was an eye-minded gentleman and as smart as they are made. "This Hite kid," Kent said, "just hasn't got it. Her walk, for instance, isn't yours. She doesn't carry herself as you do and I can't teach her. Now, Davenport might get that. He could catch on, too fast, to what's going on because *he's* reading the papers. Don't think he's not. And I'm afraid of that eye. In his own house, too. I'm nervous about it. We can't wreck this thing now."

He was nervous, all right, ready to jump out of his skin. But he did not tell Cora what really made him nervous, or anything at all about Ed Jones. He said he had changed this Los Angeles bit to a device he considered safer. So he told her what she was to do. He told her it depended on his getting in touch with Darlene. So he would signal. He told her how he would do that. If he gave the signal, she was to use the revised version. If not, then they would have to stick to the original, because they must coincide with Darlene, if she went through with it. So Cora made a note or two on her script, which was always with her. *He told her the title of a certain book and described its jacket, which she noted.* After that, she saw that the coast was clear for him, and Kent Shaw left the way he had come, and Cora joined me.

And if I suspected nothing, I truly believe, *neither did she!*

Kent Shaw flew off to Los Angeles. On the 25th, he met Darlene. She was as disguised and inconspicuous as ever. He congratulated her on her finesse, said he'd even raise her pay, said the scheme was going like wildfire and everyone was pleased with her. He must have been probing shrewdly into Darlene's emotions and sensibilities. The praise braced her but she remained cool. More money, of course, she approved.

He told her that the one unforgivable thing would be exposure of the plot, ever. He said it must remain the mystery of the decade, and never revealed. He said there had been only four people in the world who knew, four who would be forever silent. He was one, she another, and Cora, and one more. But now there was Ed Jones. Oh, he said she had done well to tell Ed Jones. He understood that. But now, he, Kent Shaw, would take over. This Jones liked money? Darlene said that he did, but he was vain and he was after *her*.

"You don't want him, do you?" Kent Shaw asked her outright. Darlene said, placidly, "No." So Kent Shaw told her not to worry. This Jones would follow her no more. She probably wouldn't see Ed Jones again.

Darlene sighed relief. It had been a strain.

Kent pried into the past. Who was Ed Jones? Darlene said she had known him in high school, where he'd never paid much attention to her.

"You don't mind what I tell him about you?" Kent asked. And Darlene said no. "New leaf?" Kent Shaw had asked suddenly and shrewdly.

"When I get the end pay," Darlene had said.

"You'll have to be careful. Remember, don't let any tax man start wondering."

Darlene implied that she'd thought of that long ago, not having been born yesterday. Then, Kent Shaw, perceiving once more her relationship with law and authority, told her he had changed the script, and what she was to do.

She was to do nothing in Los Angeles.

He was taking a risk with Darlene, but he had to. She left that city on the night of the 28th of March. She wore her little veil, her inconspicuous clothing. She spoke to no one on the bus, caught nobody's eye. She changed to a train in Reno, went east, then south, and by a roundabout route to New Orleans, where she checked in at last for a "vacation."

But by this time she knew what, I do believe, *she* had not suspected, either.

CHAPTER 8

So March went along and the Dream Walker affair seemed to be dying down. Some people pointed out that the dreams had occurred in December, January, February, and one should happen in March and Cora was watched. But nothing happened until March was nearly gone.

The night of the 28th, there were people in Cora's apartment. Mildred Garrick (who by now took a proprietary interest toward the whole thing and came as frequently as she could) was there. Charley Ives, of course, and four or five other people who do not really count. It was a gloomy Sunday. The weather was dull. People were in some kind of depressed state, longing for spring, which would tease us for weeks before it really came. The evening wasn't jelling socially. Mildred was restless and glum. She wore a black-and-silver buckle in her hair and told Charley Ives, who was kidding her, that she knew it was not a success. Mildred had a blind spot, a certain lack of humor about her famous idiosyncrasy.

Charley was sprawled all over a sofa big enough for two.

A couple of guests were quarreling bitterly without

saying a word to each other, using the rest of us as way stations for nasty cracks. One other was getting as drunk as he could, all by himself. Cora seemed irritable and almost on the point of throwing everyone out. How I wished she would!

She was wearing a violet velvet jumper with a white silk blouse and she looked very handsome. She'd put it on after I had turned up in salmon silk and we clashed so dreadfully that I couldn't sit in the room near her. So I was on the window bench, withdrawn. I was tired of living with Cora. I wished I could read. My tongue was hanging out for a book.

Cora swished over to her TV set and somebody groaned and said, "Oh no, have we come to this!"

"Don't complain," said she. "You're not being amusing." It was her house and her set and no one could stop her. She clicked around the channels and we got a snatch of one commercial after another. "What was *that?*" she said and turned back.

A panel. Everyone groaned. "Wait a minute," said Cora in a bright interested voice. "Look who's on!"

It was Kent Shaw. There he sat, hunched and tense and bouncing ever so slightly. The camera wheeled along the faces and steadied on the so-called contestant. That panel show was an imitation of its betters, originating in Hollywood, making heavy hash of a stale idea. People in Cora's room began to make wittier remarks in criticism. The great boon of television! Sometimes the wit and nonsense that flies among friends during a B-movie is more entertaining than an A-movie in a politely silent theatre could possibly be.

The camera came to Kent Shaw and he put his

thumb in his mouth, a most unfamiliar gesture, something I'd never seen him do. How could I know it was a signal?

Somebody had just made a crack about the unfortunate contestant that, to us in our low state, seemed hilarious, and there was laughter in Cora's room for the first time that evening, when she slowly toppled over from where she'd been sitting on a cushion. Cora, in violet velvet, was out on the floor.

"Is this one of *those?*" a guest said, awed and delighted.

Charley was kneeling beside her. For a big man, he can move as fast as a cat. I knelt, too, as he worked the cushion gently under her head. She was in no faint. Her pulse was quick and jumpy. It occurred to me that Cora was excited and the blood was telling us so. I could not believe in her. I had tried. I'd done my best to give her all the benefit of every trifle of doubt. But I knew she was faking.

"Where do you suppose she *is?*" a girl said, shrilly.

"Be quiet," said Mildred. "Eleven-thirty-eight, E.S.T. Who is going to take this down?"

The man who had been drinking too much looked remarkably sober and said he could do it. Mildred's cold eye didn't trust him. There was a muted dispute going on over our heads while Charley and I knelt there and Cora was still.

She was relaxed. That took control. Most trained entertainers know how to do it. I can do it, myself. I teach my girls the trick of letting every muscle go. The heart will quiet . . .

But Cora didn't stay out for more than five minutes.

88

She rolled her head, opened her eyes, and the whole room became utterly still.

"I was walking in a street or a road," she said. Charley's arm held her sitting up. "No one . . . no one was there. I could tell there were high banks or hills on both sides. The street was like a ditch, deep down. I saw a sign by a street lamp, next to a palm tree. Cameroon Canyon Drive. I crossed the cross-road. I could see lights, very high up, to my right and left. But I was down in a kind of slot. I was scared. I'm always scared." Her lips trembled. No one else in that room so much as breathed.

"I kept walking," she went on. "There was nobody . . . nobody to ask. I saw a pink house, with white frosting, number 11880 . . . 11880," she repeated. Then she screamed. "Look in the ferns! Look in the ferns!" she cried out. "In the ferns!" And she put her face into Charley's coat. She put her arms around his neck, her fingers clutching, her body shaking. I felt sick.

Mildred was bending over. "What else? Now, come on, Cora. Never mind the hysterics."

Charley said, almost absent-mindedly, "You shouldn't pester." And how he did it, I don't know, but he got up from the floor with Cora in his arms. He put her on the couch but she wouldn't let go of him. I saw him gently prying her fingers loose.

"No use to get a doctor," Mildred said disgustedly.

Cora turned. Now, her back was to the room and her face was in the upholstery. She wasn't making a sound.

89

"Cora." Mildred shook her shoulder. "Is that all, for heaven's sakes! Cora?"

Cora said the one word she shouldn't have said. She said, "Dead."

"What did she say?" No one could make anything of it and Cora lay silent with her head buried.

"Oh, let her alone," I said.

"Ollie?" She made the faintest whimper of my name.

"I'm here."

Charley got up from the edge of the couch, poker-faced, and I sat down. The salmon of my dress against the violet of hers was enough to put your teeth on edge.

"Palm tree, eh?" Mildred said. "South, then. Florida again?"

"With lights up high and a road in a canyon, it sounds like California," Charley said.

"Sooner or later," said Mildred grimly. "Oh sure. Southern California. Beverly Hills, I presume. Well, well. Let's see."

Somebody argued for Palm Springs but Mildred, rummaging in drawers, found a street map of Los Angeles. On the TV screen, Kent Shaw, with sour brilliance, was guessing something or other, when somebody finally turned it off.

Mildred Garrick got on the phone. The rest of us sat dumb and dazed and listened to her.

"This is Mildred Garrick, in New York City. A funny thing just happened here. I want to ask you to make a check on it. Can you get a man up to number 11880 Cameroon Canyon Drive? It should be a pink

90

house somewhere in your city. . . . Yes, I know. I've been there. It's quite a city and I've seen the colors of your houses. . . . Sure, I understand that in a polite way you're saying I've got a crust. . . . Listen, I called the police because I'm a law-abid . . . I work for the newspapers. . . . Because I want somebody with authority. . . . That's right. To go to this address right away and look in the ferns. . . . 11880 Cameroon Canyon Drive and how should I know what ferns? What trouble can it be? Pick up one of your telephones. . . . Nope, I can't explain. You wouldn't like it. . . . Doesn't look like Beverly Hills to me and I've got a map here. . . . Even so, don't you people speak to each other? . . . No, I *won't* call Beverly Hills. I can call a newspaper and get somebody right out there. . . . Okay. They can print the result I got out of this call, too. . . . Look in the ferns. That's right. . . . No, I'll call you back in about thirty minutes. . . . I told you, I run a column. . . . Okay."

"What could be in the ferns?" someone said.

"We may find out." Mildred looked grim and powerful. "Cora, if you want to make this really good, kid, better tell us from here what you saw in those ferns."

Cora wouldn't answer. She couldn't. I will always believe she did not know that the policemen, three thousand miles away, were finding in the ferns the dead body of a man named Edward Jones.

I've said Los Angeles was murky. It still is. I don't know, and no one will ever know, how Kent Shaw did it. *That* he did it isn't open to much doubt.

Ed Jones was killed by poison from a hypodermic needle, not a noisy way to kill a man. One could man-

91

age it in an automobile, for instance. How and when Kent Shaw got the body into the huge decorative mass of tall ferns on the front corner of Patrick Davenport's wide lot we do not know.

When Mildred called Los Angeles back in thirty minutes, even she let out a yelp. She stammered and stuttered and promised to explain. But first she turned around to tell us. "A body!" she said. Cora was still lying with her back to all, and she did not move. "The house belongs to Patrick Davenport," said Mildred, "and there is a dead man in the ferns!"

I *then* saw the ripple of shock go down Cora's violet back. So did Charley. Our eyes met.

Mildred left the phone hanging and yelled at her. "Did you see a dead body? *Did* you? Now listen, Cora, this isn't funny!"

"I . . . don't . . . remember . . . anything . . . at all . . ." sobbed Cora into the upholstery. "Go away. Everyone go away." Now, she shook and when I touched her she *was* cold.

And no wonder. Now, if never before, Cora Steffani knew her role had to be played *forever*. Kent Shaw had told her he would put an animal in the ferns. He told her not to say what kind, because he wanted to make it as bizarre as possible. A monkey, if he could find one. But he might, he said, have to make it a dog. Oh, I believe she did not know the dead animal would be man.

Kent Shaw took a risk with Cora but he had her in a terrible position. She'd made it too good. She'd said that word, "dead." And no one would doubt she'd meant a dead man.

92

I could tell she was really terrified and I had a vision of the uproar that was coming. It was Charley who said thoughtfully, "When this breaks she has got to have some seclusion. I'll call Dr. Harper."

"Now, wait a minute, Ives," Mildred said. "The cops are going to want to talk to her and you can't hide her."

"I'm going to get her into a hospital," Charley said. "Cops can talk to her there, can't they?"

"Oh, please!" Cora rolled over and pulled herself up. She was green with fright. "Yes, a hospital. I'm scared. I can't stand this. Take me to a hospital. Help me, somebody! There's something terribly wrong."

"Couldn't agree more," said Charley Ives, rather grimly. So he got her admitted. Charley Ives put her in that hospital. He had reasons, some of which I didn't divine. I thought it was wondrous kind.

So did Cora. I wonder how far Cora could see ahead.

Darlene Hite read all about it. It didn't occur to her to go to the police and tell all she knew and guessed. In the first place, to go to the police wasn't a thing she'd been trained to think of as either a duty or a pleasure. In the second place, once the police succeeded in tracing the recent whereabouts of Ed Jones and found out about a female companion who had been acting so modestly furtive that she used false names, it couldn't take them long to wonder whether she had some motive for getting rid of Mr. Jones. If the whole great hoax came out, no matter who told them, Darlene was in for it, because Ed's knowledge of the plot was a nice fat motive for her. Finally, Ed Jones had died between 8:00 and 10:00 P.M. and while Darlene had left L.A. at 8:00 P.M. she had done it inconspicuously. She'd come a long way round about. She couldn't possibly prove an alibi. And saddest of all, she had no faith that anyone in the world would help her.

What she had was a cool head. Then and there, *she* looked thoughtfully far ahead. She knew Darlene had to take care of Darlene.

CHAPTER 9

Brilliant! And what an improvement! (If you can stand where Kent Shaw stood.) Now, there was publicity, all right. Now, as Mildred Garrick put it, it wasn't funny. Now, there was talk. How *could* a woman surrounded by witnesses in her own apartment in New York City discover a body in Southern California?

But she had!

So how do you explain it?

If you insist it's a trick, she's mixed up in a murder and surely that's pretty drastic. Who would go this far to get her name in the papers?

And if it isn't a trick, what then? She dreams, and dreaming, walks? She travels in a trance with another body at her disposal? She can be two places at once? Why, then, she is at the least a witness in a murder case. Legally? The *Law* is going to allow that she was in Southern California and New York, both places, on the night of March 28th? Has she an alibi for this murder, or hasn't she? What's to prevent a woman of her talents from murdering or stealing or committing any other crime? If she's not subject to the laws of time and space, what can a judge do to her?

Cora was in the hospital, incommunicado.

Who was this dead man, the papers cried, and answered. He was a man named Edward Jones. Born and raised in San Diego. Navy. Then a drifter. Seattle, Chicago. After Chicago, had dropped out of sight. Then he might have been the man in the tavern in Chicago. *Was* he the man in the snow in Colorado? The hint of violence, there, was remembered and quoted. *Ah ha*, people cried. Then Cora Steffani, in her trance state at least, had reason for violence against this Jones. And she had killed him! But she was in New York, the tavern was in Chicago, the snow was in Colorado, and the body was in California.

How it bred talk! I don't suppose there was a hamlet in the land where the inhabitants did not ask each other's theory about the Dream Walker. And the answers!

Cora was in league with the Devil. Cora was a witch. Modern science is always rediscovering truth in old wives' tales. There *were* witches, after all. And this settled it.

Nonsense! Cora was insane. She had an insane capacity for telepathy. Science could swallow and digest that, somehow.

Nonsense! Cora was a criminal. The whole series had been only to cover up this crime. Alibi before the fact, of course. Ever read thrillers?

Nonsense! Cora Steffani had never, as far as could be discovered, even met this Edward Jones. Never been in San Diego. Or Seattle. Only briefly in Chicago. She was just an unfortunately gifted mystic, possibly a natural yogi. She was to be pitied. *She hadn't done it.*

Nonsense! She had a twin sister, unknown to herself and there was this famous correspondence between twins. *And the twin had done it.*

Nonsense! *Cora did it.* Because she was really a Martian, and Ed Jones had known that, and we are all being watched by Beings from Outer Space.

Nonsense! The whole thing is just a publicity stunt. Murder? *Oh, nonsense!*

Miss Reynolds called me into her office. "Miss Hudson, you've been close to this Cora Steffani? I believe you've even been staying with her, have you not?"

"I've known her for seventeen years, Miss Reynolds."

"She's in a hospital, now, I understand."

"Yes, Ma'am."

"Do you go to see her?"

"Of course."

Miss Reynolds pursed up her mouth until little vertical wrinkles made a mustache. "My dear, is it wise?"

"If wisdom comes into it," I began slowly.

"Oh, but surely it does. Olivia"—she didn't often call me Olivia and this was ominous—"I'm sure you must know that your influence with these girls is considerable."

"I know there is responsibility."

"You have a certain gift," she said. "They are drawn to you. Now I have thought of you as a fine

97

influence. I've congratulated the school for having on its staff a real lady. An old-fashioned term, but I can't think of another that comes so close to expressing the quality of graciousness and kindness and devotion to ideals."

"Thank you," I said, knowing perfectly well where all this buttering-up was going, "but if I abandon an old friend because she is in some rather sensational trouble, I'm afraid I wouldn't begin to deserve all that you are saying."

Miss Reynolds frowned. Then she broke down. "What's behind all this nonsense?" she wanted to know.

"I wish I could tell you. I can guess that she's gotten herself into a mess she didn't foresee. I know she is very much frightened. And I know that hardly anyone looks at her without seeing a freak, one kind or another. I don't know what to believe, Miss Reynolds, beyond that. The fact that she really is frightened. Of course, I could drop her. Let her be afraid by herself. It sounds as if it would be easy. Like drawing your skirts in close and walking away from someone who had fallen down in the mud. Maybe you wouldn't get physically dirty. I'm talking to myself, don't you see? I know I am in a strange position and I'm not entirely sure what's right to do. I'm quite aware that a teacher is an example. Perhaps you can help me, Miss Reynolds?"

She was looking more and more uneasy.

"Suppose," I said, "an old friend had done something very silly and it goes too far and something wicked enters in, and she is frightened and asks for you? Do you say, 'No. You got yourself into this mess and I wash my hands'?"

Miss Reynolds said, "I may have to fire you." But she used the slang term and her smile was warm, although somewhat rueful.

"I realize that you may," I said.

"What do you tell the girls?"

"I try to be . . . steady," I said. "I tell them that you needn't be blindly loyal, but you mustn't be blindly contemptuous, either. And when you don't really know enough to understand thoroughly, perhaps you should take the risk on the side of kindness." I could feel my occupation slipping out from under me. "I don't think that much will contaminate you, really," I said.

Miss Reynolds leaned back in her chair. "We are committed to sobriety and security, here," she said rather grimly, "but if you can hold it steady, as you put it, let's not be committed to cowardice." And she sniffed. "For a gentlewoman," she said, "you are a creature of some force. *I* was going to preach to *you*."

"Miss Reynolds," I said, "I love this work beyond almost anything else in my life. The trouble is, all teachers preach. If I don't practice, then I should resign. I'm groping along. I confess I do think Cora Steffani is something of a fraud. I think she has been lying and I'm sorry that it's so. But I don't think she is a criminal."

"And if, one day, you do?"

"Why," I said ignorantly, "I suppose I will still be sorry that it's so."

(What an ivory tower I was in! It makes me squirm

to remember. The world can't do without kindness. *Or anger, either*. And live and learn and, if I live, I will have learned.)

But I wasn't fired, that day, and I kept on seeing Cora.

Knowledge of the plot was now confined to the original four. Darlene was busy looking out for Darlene. Raymond Pankerman may have been shocked, but he was helpless. If he exposed Kent Shaw he, himself, was probably an accessory, for after all he had financed this murder. And his revenge, so close now, would be out the window. He kept silent. The thing was out of any control of his. Kent Shaw was running the show. And *he* lay low. By some definitions, at least, he was pushing madness. Perhaps he gloated. The publicity was a deluge.

All the past was dragged out, tapes, interviews, witnesses. Hysterically by the papers. Soberly, by the police. Maybe it was significant that comedians didn't touch it, based no gags upon it. People were somewhat afraid.

Cora was examined and cross-examined. But all the police got from her was the same impossible story. Dr. Harper had admitted her to the small hospital on the west side where she was to be "observed." They kept people out. She would see no one but the police, when she had to, and me when I could come. And Charley Ives, of course. (When I went to pay her hospital bills I found that Charley was taking care of them.)

I know something about her thoughts and guess more. Cora was horrified because a dead body was a plain and simple horror that even she could see. (Whereas, a dead, a murdered *reputatio*n was only part of the game she thought life was.) While she shivered in the dread that Ed Jones' death was just what it seemed to be—murder, and cold-blooded, too—still she tried to imagine that it could have been an accident. She had cut herself off from the communication point, that tea-room. Kent Shaw was still in Los Angeles, anyhow. So she waited.

What was she to do? Destroy herself? She had already hesitated too long. It seemed to her that the secret must be kept. But was that possible? There were three others who must never tell. Darlene, Cora did not know, had never seen in her life. But Darlene was being silent and Cora could guess *her* reasons and find them at least as powerful as her own. Raymond Pankerman was being silent. But she knew he wanted results, and she must have wondered if, failing his revenge, he would forever keep silent. Kent Shaw also wanted results, or he didn't get paid. Now she *knew* Kent Shaw. She knew that if she did not go on with the next step of the plot, Kent Shaw, in rage and frustration, might very possibly, in one grand gesture of self-destruction, broach the secret and destroy her, too. It looked to her as if "results" were indicated. Yet it would take tremendous nerve to go on.

I think she wavered. She began to feel fairly safe, protected as she was, with no assaults upon her nerves but those that came in print. And I was standing by, and Charley Ives. . . . Why not leave off, neither tell nor continue? Simply stop, now, and let there be no more of it? For the build-up was over. The next step was the big one, against Marcus. And Marcus was dearly beloved of Charley and me. She must have weighed the benefits of our partisanship against her fear of what Kent Shaw might do. I know when she decided which way to take the risk.

This Bud Gray, this big quiet man I'd met once before, became very much interested in the whole affair. One day I was in the tiny shop one could enter from the ground floor of the hospital, a convenient little corner where a visitor to the sick could find a gift, a magazine, or a snack. Charley came in with Mr. Gray.

Charley and I had been avoiding most gingerly any discussion of Cora and her behavior. I'd said I wouldn't talk behind her back and Charley scrupulously respected my decree. But Bud Gray had no such inhibition. They climbed up on stools on either side of me. "She let you in, too, eh?" Gray said to me. I nodded. "Have you tried to get her to talk?"

"No. I haven't."

"Don't you think you should?"

"Cousin Ollie thinks Cora needs a friend who won't ask questions," Charley said.

"Who doesn't?" Bud Gray remarked. "But we'd like to know who killed a man." They both looked down at me.

"If she wants to tell me anything," I murmured, "she knows she can."

"Would you respect her confidence?"

"Why, not if it was murder," I muttered.

"Then she won't tell you it was murder."

"She won't because she certainly didn't murder anyone," I said. "I was *there*."

"What *do* you think is going on, Miss Hudson?"

I shook my head. I'd been feeling trapped and miserable for days.

Gray said, "I'll tell you what I think. I think she's got an accomplice and the accomplice put the body in the ferns. I think that's obvious. Cora could tell us where to find her. Not telling us constitutes accessory after the fact."

"That's right," said Charley.

"Not telling *you*," I exploded. "Are you policemen?"

Gray smiled. I was looking at his face. But I could tell that Charley's eyes were flicking messages over my head and I nearly fell off the stool. Suddenly, I was sure that Bud Gray *was* a policeman in some fashion and I thought it must be some very secret fashion, too.

"Let's say this crazy affair has got me fascinated," Gray said. "And murder, to coin a phrase, is everybody's business, isn't it?"

I'd been having a soda. I gnashed my straw.

"Now, look here, Miss Hudson. Somebody has got to break that woman down. You wouldn't condone a murder, or so you said."

"Of course I wouldn't," I said. "But I don't *know* that Cora had anything to do . . ."

The two of them were silent for a moment.

"She has to know," said Charley.

"Did you know your friend Cora was pretty pink some years ago?" Gray asked rather tartly. "How do you stand on that sort of thing?"

"Where I think I should," I said haughtily. "What did she *do?* What is she *doing,* now? I'd have to know quite a lot about it and see some evidence before I'd take a stand."

"You see, my cousin Ollie never, never judges people without full knowledge," Charley said gently. His voice had an undertone that made me turn and his look made tears of humiliation start in my eyes.

"Are you a policeman, Charley, my boy?" I said in my most teacherish voice, to cover what I was feeling. Charley said nothing, but I felt light bursting and searing me, too.

"Charley gets around," said Bud Gray very lightly. But it seemed to me that they had told me, these two big men who *worked* at something while I, and so many others, slept. I was crying to myself, Why haven't I known! Charley in Europe after the war, Charley in Japan, wasn't in the front lines all that time. *Of course,* he was a policeman, in some secret way, and couldn't tell. (He must have promised!) I was ready to weep that I'd been so stupid.

"How p-pink is she?" I stammered. "What is it? Tell me."

Charley leaned his head on one hand. "Bud thinks he can needle you. He doesn't know you. About Cora, I can give you an opinion. She was fashionably pink, in the old days when that was fashionable. So much you probably remember, too. But in my opinion, Cora never really held a political thought in her head and never will. She belongs to a profession that doesn't always have much connection with reality. She thought it was the smart thing. Then when the style changed, she changed her ideas just as she would have changed her hem line. I will say that at one time she was ac-

104

quainted with some who weren't so superficial. But she doesn't see them any more."

I felt *furious* with Charley Ives, just as you would feel if you'd scolded a person for lying abed on a sunny day, and then found out he hadn't mentioned his broken leg. And I resented his crack about the profession. I believed that theatre people, like any artists, had to be *more* alert and *more* informed about reality than anybody else. At which, of course, *I'd* failed, not to know that Charley Ives was up to something! *Everything* was humiliating.

"Put it plain, then," said Gray. "Do you think Cora Steffani would talk to you?"

I suppose, to keep the silly tears from spilling over, I made my face proud. With some effort I considered what he was saying. I shook my head. "We are not confidantes, as you can see. Besides, I'm not cut out to be a spy."

Charley said, "It's not high-minded, is it, teacher?" His big shoulders heaved. (We were fighting.) "Acting, on the stage, you see, Bud, that's Art. But in real life, it's something sneaky and low."

"*Everybody* acts, in real life," I said. "And sometimes it's sneaky and sometimes it's self-control. And nobody's talking about Art."

"Let's not be sneaky," he said as if he hadn't heard me. "Let murder go."

Gray said, "We *were* talking about murder, weren't we? Well, Charley, I guess I was wrong. I thought she might help us. Never mind," he said to me. "It isn't any job for a lady school teacher."

I was so mad I could hardly see. "You were married

105

to Cora once, Charley, my boy," I said coldly, "and might as well be, now. Aren't *you* in her confidence? Why can't *you* break her down? *You* should know how."

Charley's face wasn't saying anything. "Maybe you're right, Teacher. Maybe I better go up," Charley said, "and in my own crude way, do what I can."

He left us, not so much as looking backward, and Mr. Gray and I sat side by side.

"I suppose he's very good at it," I sniffed forlornly.

"Who's good at what?"

"Charley Ives. At this secret kind of police job."

"What job? I don't know what you're talking about?" Bud Gray wasn't going to tell me anything. He moved his soft-drink glass in slow circles. "Charley's a good citizen, shall we say?"

"Oh certainly. That's what we'll say," I said from the depths and blew my nose.

"It's the bizarre, the time-and-space angle, that fascinates me about this business," Gray said ruminatively. "Practically makes a Federal Case out of it." He grinned. "But the other woman must be plenty smart."

"The other?" I made myself stop thinking about Charley Ives.

"The accomplice. The one who does the walking, on schedule, and then vanishes. The one people see. Her job isn't easy." He spoke with a good deal of sympathy. I suppose he's had experience and knows what it means to turn up on schedule, and to vanish, too.

"How could there be such a person? How can they do all this?"

"Ah," said Gray, "we wish we knew."

"And why?" said I. But I wasn't really wondering why. I was worrying only about my own position. How could I turn away from Cora? And how could I not? What should I do? Now, I can understand that nobody expected me to be superhumanly wise. But me. Which was pretty vain and foolish, but there I floundered.

When Charley came down in about five minutes, he wore his poker face. They both went away, saying only polite good-bys. I felt cast out.

I went up to Cora's room and found her in a weeping rage. Charley Ives had made her so. Who else? So I proceeded to be patient and soothing toward the furious woman whom I even tried to forgive for taking some of her anger out in sullen unresponsiveness to me. But whom I neither knew, nor understood nor even deeply cared for. No harm if, passively, in suspension of judgment, I stood by an old friend, said I to myself, compulsively.

That's when she decided to go through with it. She had compulsions of her own. Marcus says the difference between us was only that she didn't take the risk on the side of kindness. But I think Marcus is kind.

107

CHAPTER 10

The whole month of April went by with Cora barricaded, everybody baffled, hue and cry. Nothing more happened until that 5th day of May.

Darlene, meanwhile, was going about her business. Kent Shaw stayed out west. He was not seen about, and certainly not thought about by me. Raymond Pankerman was in the throes, now, and his case competed with Cora's in the headlines.

And Cora remained in that hospital, acting, acting. Doctors came and went. Policemen came and went. Before all of these, she remained stubbornly baffled, herself, afraid of her own mystery, and unable to remember (*that* neat device that saved her so much trouble and risk) any more than was on record already about her dreams.

And I came and went, in the delusion that I was aloof but kind, and I found Cora listless, playing prostration. We would speak idly of other things. I must have been restful. But Charley Ives came no more. I did not see him, anywhere.

Now a day or so after Cora's stormy time with Charley Ives, she had a jeering little note from Kent

Shaw. I brought her mail from her apartment. She let me read the note. It said:

> *Cora, darling:*
>   Dead bodies, aw-ready! Come off it, why don't you? Next time you get on your broom, keep away from Los Angeles. This kind of town, a man takes too much dope some night, they clean the streets. Me, I don't believe all I read in the papers. When I do, send me rue, send me rosemary.
>
> *Kent*

I made nothing of that. Maybe Cora saw both a re-assurance and a threat in it. And took rosemary for re-membrance. She *wanted* to believe Kent Shaw was not a killer. And she knew nothing about Ed Jones, except what had been in the papers. Nobody *knew* he was the man in Chicago, or in the snow. That was only guess-work. Maybe she could believe that Kent Shaw, look-ing for something dead, had found a body. Just any body. Maybe she swallowed that. In a way, she had to. Anyhow, the public uproar continued.

It was bad for the hospital. Cora thought it was a fortress, but it was her prison. Charley Ives had put her there to keep, and the hospital, resenting it fiercely, was nevertheless stuck with her. So she spread herself out in that room-and-bath, bringing her own things, becoming cozy. But newspapermen crept about the building, trying to get in and the open pressure they put on was enough nearly to buckle the walls. Cora kept refusing to see the Press.

On the 4th day of May, she capitulated. She agreed

109

to talk to one and chose Ned Dancer for that one because she knew him. He could relay the interview, or not, as he pleased. (He'd better please, said the rest.) She would see him tomorrow, at 2:00 P.M. if Dr. Harper and I would consent to be present.

So then it was the 5th of May, and at 2:00 P.M., Ned was ceremoniously admitted, and along with him who should turn up but Charley Ives.

"Mind?" he said.

Cora said wanly and sweetly, "Of course not, Charley. Please do stay." If there was a glitter in the eyes, the lids were heavy and hid it. I didn't sense the malice. I was busy taking care to be calm and detached in my chosen position, standing by.

I will not forget that fifth incident. The scene exists somewhere indelibly in my brain as if it were a film in a can. It actually does exist on a piece of tape, for anyone to hear again. Ned Dancer had brought the inevitable recorder. Cora made no objection. Ned said there were some people who didn't trust him, as he plugged it into the wall and set the microphone on the table.

Cora was propped high on the bed, having climbed back in to play invalid for this occasion. She wore a rose-pink woolly bed jacket and careful make-up. Set among her froth, that could not entirely conceal the hospital white and hospital austerity, she was rosily and frivolously pretty, except for the pawn-of-fate mask on the face and the nervous slide of the hands along the edge of the sheet, back and forth. Ned Dancer stood up to the right of her and asked his questions in his unemotional voice. The doctor, a tubby little man with graying hair en brosse, rimless glasses, and an air of harassed good will, was silently standing behind him.

Charley Ives was sprawled in the low visitor's chair, overflowing it, not so much physically, as by the very quality he has of being noticeable. I had refused that chair or any. I was literally standing by, on Cora's left. I remember my dress because I wore it for days afterwards, a crisp taffeta with white at neck and cuff (which white I laundered in some odd places).

Cora answered Ned's questions patiently and without fire. There was nothing new. We'd heard these answers all before. The interview went drearily as the tape rolled relentlessly on the spool. At half past two, Dr. Harper shifted position, as Cora's eyes closed tiredly. "About enough . . ." he began.

"One or two more," Ned begged, "and then I'd like to talk to *you,* Doctor."

"Nothing I can tell you," Dr. Harper said quickly putting up his defenses. I was listening to this exchange.

Charley rose from the chair. Cora's head had slipped sideways. I stood there and saw the flutter of her heart expressed in trembling pink wool and I thought, appalled, "Oh no, no, no! Not again! Not any more!"

The doctor stepped closer. Ned Dancer said, "What?" Then sharply, "Is that a trance state, Doctor?"

Dr. Harper touched her. His lips tightened. He lifted a hand to slap her cheek and Ned stopped him. "Wait," he begged. "Let's just see what happens. This is giving me a break." His bleak eyes commented: Break, yah! No doubt my presence was arranged. He looked around at the spool of tape still turning. "How long do these things last?"

Charley said, "Can you tell she's faking, Doc? What about it?"

Dr. Harper licked his lip. When he spoke he must have had the turning tape in mind, because it was a fine screen of obscuring syllables, sounding calm and judicious, but with no meaning. He didn't even commit himself to saying he didn't know.

Ned said anxiously, "That's an hour's tape and there's about twenty minutes left. What do you think? Shall I turn it off? I want to *get* this and I'd rather not stop it. How many minutes do these fits run?"

"You want a prophecy?" said Charley, somber and resigned.

Dr. Harper forgot his caution. "I can bring her out of that, I think." I knew at once he had pain in mind.

"No, no," said Ned. "Wait a minute. Listen . . ." he wanted the story. (May he be forgiven.)

"Sit down, Ollie," Charley said to me. "You don't have to stand there, for gosh sakes. You look like you're going to fall down."

"I'm all right," I said, trying not to fall against his arm. But I wasn't all right. I did need supporting. I was tired to death of the whole business. How long could I stand by while this went on? How long was Cora (my old friend Cora) going to keep it up? At first, I was weary. Then, I was afraid. It seemed too long, too much, too elaborate. She'd got all the publicity possible, already. She was in a mess about a murder. What more did she want? How *could* it go on?

What if, I thought, Cora really was helpless, was ill in the sense of being abnormal, supernatural? Then, was it a shell, lying there in pink, and did Cora herself, clothed in a spare body, like a second suit of clothes, walk somewhere? Speak somewhere? To be seen and heard somewhere else, not here?

To believe that *all this was contrived* seemed just as mad as to believe it wasn't. For the first time, really, I, Olivia Hudson, tasted belief in the appearances. It was the first time and the last.

The clock and the tape rolled on and on with our heart beats, Charley's, where the back of my head was resting, mine near where his hand held me. Time played tricks with me, being very long, very short. It was actually twelve minutes before Cora opened her eyes and straightened her neck and stiffened her back.

Ned glanced at the tape, still going, and was about to speak when I said (may I be forgiven), "Don't interrupt. She forgets, if you do."

Cora said in that brisk way she had of speaking her part, so effective, because it sounded like simple reporting with all her emotions postponed. "I was walking. I was in a park. Wearing my gray coat. I stopped to . . . see where I was. There was a man on the path who said to me, 'Beg pardon, could I ask a favor of a stranger?' He wasn't young, wasn't old. I *knew* him." Cora pressed her temples in her palms. She had the stage. Not one of us moved. "He said to me," she went on, " 'Would you give this envelope to an old gentleman around the corner, sitting on a bench, over

113

there? Just tell him it's from Ray.' 'I'll be glad to,' I said, 'if you will tell me where I am.' 'You are in Washington,' he told me. 'Just do this thing for me?' So I walked around the corner and there was an old gentleman and I gave him the envelope. It was pale blue. And I said, 'This is from Ray.' And he thanked me and put it away. So I . . ." She hesitated.

Charley's hands hurt me. Charley said in a quiet voice but one that vibrated through my whole body, "Who was the old gentleman?"

"Marcus," said Cora at once, staring into space. "John Paul Marcus."

"And this Ray?"

"I've seen his picture all over," she said. "I think the name is Pankerman. So I . . ."

"What's this?" Ned's eyes jumped.

Cora looked bewildered. Her eyes changed focus. "I don't know," she faltered.

"That's all for now?" said Charley in that same voice.

"It fades," she whimpered.

"The hell it fades—" Charley threw me aside and went over and jerked out the cord of the tape recorder.

"Let it alone," bellowed Ned Dancer. "Wait a minute. Cora, *what did Marcus do with the envelope?*"

Cora opened her mouth but didn't speak. Charley was stuffing the cord into the recorder's case with violent haste. He discarded the microphone. He shut down the lid. Ned said, "Hey, that's mine."

Charley said, "Dancer, if you breathe . . ."

Ned said, "I got to."

114

"Come to Washington. You can't print this kind of stuff without checking."

"No," Ned said.

"And you won't." Charley wasn't asking.

"I will, if it checks," Ned said. "I got to."

Charley said, "Doc, keep quiet and shut her up. Don't let anybody in here."

"Nurse . . ."

"Keep the nurses quiet." Charley yanked out Cora's telephone. The doctor yelped. "The woman's a devil," said Charley Ives. "I'd strangle her, gladly, right now. If it would do any good. Which it wouldn't. You, keep her quiet." Cora began to wail and moan. Charley now had the tape recorder in one hand and Ned's shoulder in the other. "Cousin Ollie," he barked at me. "You better keep her lying mouth shut."

"Get out of here," the doctor said wearily.

Ned Dancer opened the door. The doctor was bending over his writhing patient with his ear close. We didn't hear it. We were not meant to hear it yet. But she told him, then or a little later, one thing more.

I didn't hear it because I went out the door behind the men. "It's all lies," I said in the corridor.

Charley sucked air in through his teeth. I'd never seen him so angry, not even the time we had fought so long ago. "Raymond Pankerman passing secret papers to *Marcus!*" Charley made a sound of such deep disgust that I thought he had spit on the floor.

"It's going to check," Ned Dancer said. "Marcus himself is going to tell us there was this dame in a gray coat . . ."

115

"That he accepted an envelope from some stranger? From some Ray? Naaaaah."

"And put it away. Yes, and it will be found."

"Can't be."

"No? Dead body couldn't be in the ferns, either. This thing is built."

"Over my dead body will they get away with this one," Charley said.

I said, "Tell me what I can do."

Charley herded us both down the hall into Dr. Harper's office. He closed and locked the door and got on the phone. Ned stood there biting his thumbnail, his cold eyes bleak. I stood against the door.

"Ruthie? . . . Charley Ives." Now Ned moved and listened to little Ruthie Miller's voice from Washington. "Where is Marcus? . . . Oh, yes, I see. . . . Anybody with him? . . . Cunneen, eh? No, nothing I can tell you. Just ask Marcus not to talk to anybody outside the household. Tell him I'm coming right down."

"So he's in the park?" said Ned.

"Yes, he's in the park. It's a chilly day, but he goes if it isn't actually storming." Charley was quoting. His mouth drew down bitterly.

He dialed Long Distance again. Maybe you've seen a man fight with a telephone for his weapon. Charley argued, insisted, demanded, and finally, although it had taken him twenty minutes, he got a number out of someone that gave him the man he was after.

"I want to talk to Raymond Pankerman," said Charley for the sixth time. "I'm told he's due there. . . . This is Charley Ives and it *is* important. . . .

116

Oh, he did? Put him on. . . . I don't care what he wants to know. Tell him who is calling." Charley hung on.

Ned Dancer lifted his head. "He's been in the park?" said he lightly, like the flick of a rapier.

"Yes, he's just come across the park," said Charley's bitter mouth. He was hunched over the phone with one foot on the recorder. I stood tight against the door. Ned moved up and down like a man in a cell. Then once more he put his ear where he, too, could hear the speaker on the wire.

"Pankerman? My name is Ives. You crossed the park just now? . . . As a matter of fact, I *am* interested. You met a woman in a gray coat? . . . No, I *don't* need to tell you what it's all about. Did you give her anything? . . . What's that? . . . *Go to hell!*" shouted Charley and hung up and held his head. Ned Dancer said something crude and unfit for my ear.

"What did he say?" I quavered.

"He said he didn't have to answer," said Charley in a voice of loathing. "Asked me if I'd ever heard of the Fifth Amendment?"

We stared at each other's faces.

(Oh, how deep was Raymond Pankerman's prankish laughter? How much did the ego expand under the tweeds? How sweet was his revenge?)

Charley jumped up, pushed me aside and unlocked the door. He herded us out, seeming as big as a mountain and about as lazy and easygoing as a volcano.

"Tell me how to help," I cried. "What shall I do?"

Charley had no hands. He hung onto that recorder and Ned's shoulder again and Ned was as shifty and

117

nervous as a race horse at the barrier. "You, Teacher?" Charley was thinking about everything but me. "I got to get hold of Gray. Ned and I are going to Washington, right quick. Find the accomplice. Get the whole damn scheme out by the roots. Prove exactly how they are working this." He spun around.

"I'll try," I said.

Charley gave me one blue flash through his lashes. Then they were off, taking the stairs, looking for an escape from what other newsmen might be lurking in the lobby. They went too fast for me to follow.

I knew, as well as Charley did, how this could hurt Marcus. What, *he* had any furtive truck at all with such as Pankerman? If such a thing were rumored, the whole country would wince and ask an explanation.

Rumored! But the *way* of this rumor was so fantastic! There was no explanation of Cora Steffani, the Dream Walker. No way to understand how she could have done what she said she did in that park. But oh, there would be people to swear that Pankerman was in the park, at the exact right time. And Cora had done it before, as the whole world thought it knew. There was a dead man in the ferns, wasn't there? So some would dismiss this for a ridiculous falsehood, and some would not. But fraud or no fraud, not one cranny of the nation could fail to reverberate with the *story*. Marcus would be in the white heat of publicity, defensive, trying to prove a negative, denying.

Denying what? We didn't even know yet what was supposed to be in the envelope, but I quaked to think of it. Ned Dancer must be right. There would be an envelope. The devilish scheme would include a real

118

envelope, somehow, somewhere. It wasn't all clear in my head, but I *felt* that here was the reason for the whole scheme. I felt they meant to injure Marcus and this purpose was important enough for all the trouble.

Charley Ives was right. The one thing to be done was expose. Get it out. Open it. Find out who, how, why, and tell, on our side, with fact, fact, and fact. We could not sit smug and say, "Why that's ridiculous. Untrue. Who could believe such nonsense!" People didn't have to believe the nonsense. Doubt was enough. Doubt, for most, is exactly the same thing as condemnation. Those who are really able to suspend judgment are not in the majority. Even they aren't getting anywhere, but only preparing to get somewhere.

I saw all this. I could no longer stand around piously maintaining that I hadn't enough to go on, so I wasn't making up my mind. *Harm* was being done. You can't just tolerate cruelty, *un*kindness. You have to *find* something to go on. I gave up being inhumanly detached. I was just as human as anybody else. I took some things on faith. I chose my side. That's not enough, either. I must go *find proof* that the Dream Walker was a wicked fraud.

I went downstairs and talked the hospital into cashing a big check. I wasn't a policeman. I had to do what *I* could do.

I called on Josephine Crain.

CHAPTER 11

"Jo," I said, "I'm here to beg you to help me prove that Cora Steffani is a fraud and this business a hoax."

"Well!" Josephine's lovely eyes were amused. She drew me down on a quaint little sofa in her sunny room. "What's happened, Olivia? I thought you were her little soldier." (I hoped she'd never have to know what had happened.) "Not that I don't agree with you," Jo added. "She's used me and I don't like that. Never did."

"Tell me about the woman on the beach. She wasn't Cora, of course. How was she *different?*"

"I don't like to talk about it and don't quote me, Ollie, or I'll scream." Jo looked at me thoughtfully. "But there was one thing that nobody seems to have noticed. In her little scene, *I had no lines.*"

"Charley Ives noticed that."

"Bright lad. Look, Ollie, my dear, I saw her for the briefest moment. I hardly got my attention out of my book. She resembles this Cora, of course. It's the same nose."

"I want a difference."

Jo said, "I've seen this Steffani on TV, you know."

"Go on, Jo. You did notice something."

"The woman I saw on the beach didn't use her hands. Whereas Steffani is the handy kind," Jo made with beautiful accuracy one of Cora's flying gestures. "That's a deep habit, a mannerism like that." She looked at me sideways.

"Doesn't help much, unless you're ready to swear."

"*I'm* convinced," Jo shrugged. "But what would it mean if I did swear?"

"Was she excited?"

"Not very. A cool customer, I'd say. I think she intended to seem upset and confused. But her hands didn't move, Ollie."

I sat thinking of Cora's hands, acting out annoyance, anguish, bewilderment, anything, everything.

"Every hair on your head says this is important," Jo smiled. "Don't tell me why, if I shouldn't know."

"I need some proof. I need it bad. Tell me this, Jo. You do go to the beach as a regular thing? People could expect you to be there?"

"I go south for the sun and I insist on it. Yes, I sit on the beach and read or study every day that it is possible and nobody disturbs me. Yes, it's regular. I daresay I am as good as a sundial."

"That's why they used *you*," I said.

"It seems to me they've used you, too," she reminded me.

"Jo, if you think of anything . . ."

"If I had proof," she said tartly, "I'd have trotted it out long ago."

I rose and she was willing to let me leave her as abruptly as I wished. I was thinking that surely Josephine Crain's opinion would have some weight. Josephine Crain's conviction would convince. Then at her door she said, "Wait a minute. There was a ring on her right hand. A narrow dark stone."

121

My hope ebbed away. An observant woman, an honest woman, who was an expert on gesturing hands, who understood the tyranny of a deep habitual mannerism. So what? It was the ring that would count. Cora Steffani wore on her right hand a ring with a narrow stone.

Angelo Monti I tracked down (learning from Charley Ives) by wrestling for an hour over the telephone. He was in town and at rehearsal.

"Miss Hudson," he said, reluctantly, "I can tell you only that I saw the woman. I saw Cora Steffani. They looked like one to me. I am short-sighted. My vision is not all that it ought to be. Perhaps I am not a good eye-witness. I hope not."

"They are two women and I must find the one you saw in Chicago."

He didn't argue with me. He had soft brown eyes, and whether they could see well or not, they were sympathetic. "I wish I could help you," he said. "You are very determined, for some reason."

"Any smallest thing . . ." I thought to myself he was a kind of expert, too. "Her voice?"

"Her ordinary voice," said Monti, "is a little bit nasal. Not bad. Not good."

"*Cora*'s isn't."

"Is that true?"

"But did you never hear Cora speak?"

"I hear her on the air. Then it is the actress voice. Too high in the mouth to my taste. I think it is like some singers who have the worst dreadful speaking voice in this world. They do not use their expensive education for every day, eh?"

"*Cora* does," I insisted.

"Ah? But this woman spoke to me in Chicago with a nasal voice. Oh, very faint, but unpleasant to me. If she was lost, you know, to be unhappy will change the voice." He was getting vague and confused. I wondered if he were superstitious.

"But you'd be willing to say the voice in Chicago is not the voice Cora uses on stage?"

"That much, I would say. My ear is good. Does this have a meaning?"

"Wait," I said. "You saw Cora herself, here in New York. Didn't she *speak* to you?"

"She did not," Monti said. "It was in a studio. I was arriving and she leaving. I did not speak much myself, only to say her name. What does one say to someone you have met in her dream? It is awkward. She looked quickly very unsteady and her friends led her away. Perhaps it was odd that she did not speak *at all*." He looked at me hopefully.

"I think it was odd," I said.

"My eyes can be fooled. My ear, no. I guess you are pretty, Miss Hudson. I *know* your voice is charming and I would recognize it in the dark twenty years from now."

"I'm sure you would," I said warmly. He was such a nice worried kind little man. "But the problem is to find this faintly nasal voice." He shrugged, looking helpless. "Tell me this, Mr. Monti. Could it be predicted that you would be in that tavern, that night?"

So then he explained about his friend, Gallo.

"I see. I see. Yes, that's helpful. You were bound to be there and nowhere else. They could count on it."

"This helps you believe there are two women. But does it prove so?"

"No. No, of course not."

"The man," said Monti, "I have identified in a picture." He shivered delicately.

"What picture?"

"A picture of the dead man in Los Angeles. Of course, I don't trust my eyes. I cannot hear his voice again, unhappily."

"The dead man *was* the same man! The police have talked to you?" I cried.

"Have they not." He sighed.

"Did you mention the woman's voice to them?"

"No one asked. I did tell them one more thing, not in the papers."

"What was that?"

"She wore a pin. Gallo, my friend, he agrees to this. It was a small golden horse pinned on her shoulder. Gallo has eyes."

"Yes," I said, my excitement fading. "I mustn't keep you."

I left him. There it was again. An expert, a man with a delicate ear. But who would trust these experts of mine? And their intangibles? Cora's golden horse, for sale in department stores everywhere, it was solid. It would count.

I called Miss Reynolds and begged a leave of absence. I suppose my urgency was as obvious over the phone as it was in Jo's sitting room or the bleak rehearsal hall. She let me go. I caught a cab, all luggageless as I was, to the airport. There are not many seasons when a single person, both flexible and determined, cannot get a seat to where she wants to go. In an hour I was on a plane for Denver.

I had two little details about the second woman. She

124

did not use her hands much when she talked and she talked in a voice that was faintly nasal to a very discriminating ear. What, I asked myself, would Dr. Barron of Denver be an expert about? I found out very soon.

It was dark when I got to Denver and late by the time I had myself dumped on his doorstep. In one of Denver's inevitable brick houses, I met the gentleman whose voice I already knew.

"Is there anything at all I can do for you?" he said to me.

"My name is Olivia Hudson. I've come from New York. I need your help."

"Why, then, you'll surely have it," said he, and he took me in and the first thing I knew I was sipping hot tea while the good man's wife, who was a little bit of a dumpling with snowy hair and merry young eyes, would not listen to any tale of having been fed on an airplane but prepared to give me nourishment as if I were starving.

I told Dr. Barron all about the Washington incident. He reminded me of Marcus. Although he was a foot taller and perhaps a foot wider, too, he was just as solid all through.

"It's a dirty business, then," said he. "Bearing false witness like that. Now, how shall I help you, my dear?"

"Think of something," said I once more, "that distinguishes those two women. To help me find the other one. Did the one on the path use her hands much?" I made Cora's gestures. "Like this?"

"Maybe she didn't." Dr. Barron's beautiful clear gray eyes were intent on the memory of what he had seen.

"Or the voices. Were they different?"

"It's possible. I never swore they were one. After a while, I was not satisfied."

"Why weren't you, sir?"

"Now, the one that met me on the path," said he, "*that one* was making out to be lost." He looked me in the eye. "But it was all put-on," he said.

"You mean she was acting?"

"Put-on," he repeated. "It wasn't true. If ever I saw a young woman who'd know where she was, and all, it was *that one*. She was not a bit scared and she didn't think she was doing wrong."

"What do you mean?"

"A fellow in my line of work, he meets more of sin and sorrow than the baker's boy," said Dr. Barron, "and she wasn't sinning and she wasn't sorry. She was cool as a cucumber and it might be that she was doing her duty. But the young lady who came the following day, oh, she was mad."

"Cora was *mad?*"

"Full of the anger and the hatred. And the weeping and the gnashing of teeth," he said. "Oh, but that was put-on. And me trying to comfort her when they turned the machine off, and she tickled to death about something all the time. Indeed, she was."

I realized his field, in which he was an expert. Soul states, you might call it. I gasped. "You mean Cora was triumphant? But of course, she might have been." I began to turn in my mind my own memories of Cora's states. I'd known her for seventeen years. All I remembered sensing under the mask was a bit of malice, now and then. But of course Cora was malicious. Always had been. I was just used to it.

"Oh, she wasn't so easy," Dr. Barron said, "until I had said my say and she was sure it pleased her. Oh, that weeping and that wailing and that gnashing of teeth, it was put-on all right." (And he'd know what was put-on. I couldn't doubt it.) "Sorry," said he, "*she* was not. But she was sinning. For I count it not a good sound thing to be full of hate for another. Now, the young man, Charley. He was one she's mad at."

"Oh?" I said faintly. "You mean my cousin, Charley Ives? Why, I guess they quarreled. But Cora doesn't hate Charley. They were married once, but it was a friendly divorce."

Dr. Barron looked at me kindly. "Did you think there was such a thing, my dear?"

"But *tell* me . . ."

"Now, my dear, what am I to tell you? That young woman would enjoy the clawing of his bright blue eyes out. And if she plays she wouldn't, it's only put-on. How can I know why that is? But here we're doing no better than gossiping and we're no farther."

"It's hardly proof," I said, feeling very queer. I pulled myself together. "Dr. Barron, did the police ever show you a picture of Edward Jones?"

"He that leapt out into the path, the day, and grabbed her? They did, indeed, show me a picture but I was too far. If he's the man who's dead, I should be sorry I did not swear it was *two* young women, at the time."

"I don't know how much good it would have done," I murmured.

"It's kind of you to comfort me," said that darling man. But he needed nobody's comfort. He was *tough*, my Dr. Barron, in the most wonderful way.

"Now, here's Jane," he said, "and you'll have the dish of soup she's fixed and the bite or two on top of that and you'll spend what's left of the night on the couch which I'm told is fair comfortable."

"I can't spend the night, thank you. I requested a seat to Los Angeles, and if they've got one for me, I must go. I haven't much time."

Mrs. Barron said, "Ah, dear, can you sleep on them planes so up in the air as they are?"

Dr. Barron said with the most wonderful smile, "Why not? I see, my dear, you mean to find out what is behind it all. You are very angry with these women."

"Yes," I said. "I am very angry."

"Good," said he.

But I wasn't going to put on anything. "I don't know . . . I don't care if it's good or not," I said, nearly in tears. "If I can I'm going to stop them."

"I thought I would tell you," he said gently, "it's not always a bad thing to be angry. For I can see you are not used to it. Eat now, while I'm thinking if there is anything at all that I can do."

He hadn't remembered anything more before I found the airline had a seat for me and I left them in a rush, but feeling as if I were tearing myself away from my home. While I was borne in the dark over the mountain snow and over the desert cold, I had the deepest conviction that their prayers rode with me. So I lay in my seat and I cried a little bit. And I felt better.

Although all I had found out about Darlene Hite was her hands, her voice, and the business-like state of her soul.

CHAPTER 12

Much bedraggled, I got to Los Angeles in the morning, took the airport bus to a hotel downtown and checked in, but not to rest. I washed my travel-dingy collar and cuffs which (being nylon) dried while I washed myself.

There was nothing in the papers about Marcus, not yet. I didn't call Washington or try to tell Charley Ives where I was or why. I had nothing very solid to offer. I considered where to begin here. As I dressed, I thought of renting a car and driving out to Cameroon Canyon. But I realized there was no point in talking to Patrick Davenport. He hadn't, according to all accounts, seen or heard anything whatsoever outside his house the night of the murder. I knew he was a lean, dynamic man who dominated, wherever he was, talked very fast, and was impossible to interrupt. I didn't think it would help to tangle with him.

So I went to the police.

I was put into the presence of a sober, spruce young man, Sergeant Bartholomew. He had a plain face, a steady eye, a clear soft voice, and he seemed to carry responsibility quietly, as a matter of course, although I soon felt him to be both sensitive and subtle. He repeated my name politely and I knew at once that he recognized it and me, and had placed me. I told him I'd come from New York to talk about the murder of Ed Jones. "I want you to tell me things," I said. "I don't suppose you will, unless I tell you some things first."

"It might be a good idea," he said with a smile.

So I told him all about the fifth dream, in the hospital, and Cora and Raymond Pankerman and the blue envelope. I knew I'd have to and I knew it was safe to do so. I didn't have to argue the implications. His plain face grew stern.

"Marcus is my great uncle," I said, "but you know Marcus, too, and this weird lie they are telling must be exposed. I don't know what's going on in Washington. I've been talking to Josephine Crain, and Angelo Monti and Dr. Barron, so far. Now, I want to find out from you . . ." I couldn't state what I wanted to find out.

"We want to find out, too," said he. "Did those people tell you anything useful?"

"There are *two* women, Mr. Bartholomew. There must be. And all these people think so." I told him what I had gleaned. So little. "No proof," I ended.

He was smiling over Dr. Barron. "Oh," he said easily, "there are two women, all right. The other one is the one we are looking for, too."

"You think she killed Ed Jones?"

"We think she'll know a lot about it."

"Angelo Monti identified Ed Jones, didn't he?"

"He more or less did. We have to be careful about a single identification from a photograph by a man with poor eyes."

130

"I suppose so," I said somewhat dejectedly.

He looked directly at me. "This Cora Steffani wasn't in any trance state on the night of March 26th, was she?"

"No. Why?"

"Ed Jones was seen in a bar with a woman that night."

"Here in Los Angeles? Was she like Cora?"

"The description's not very detailed. She probably was the right height and coloring."

"Nobody saw a woman on Cameroon Canyon Drive, the night of the 28th, when Cora *said* she walked there in the dream?"

"Nobody."

"Patrick Davenport didn't?"

"He sure wishes he had," grinned the Sergeant. "He's called me up six times with queer noises to report that he's just remembered and so on." He shook his head. "Nobody saw her, Miss Hudson. She wasn't there."

"Of course Cora wasn't there."

"Neither was her double. I don't think any slight five-foot-four woman—that's your own build, Miss Hudson—dragged a big man's body out of a car into those ferns." (I suppose I shuddered.) "I wouldn't be surprised if the accomplice had an accomplice," he said, watching to see what I would make of this.

"Do you know anything about this double?" I pleaded.

"I don't know whether I do." He gave me that direct and thoughtful look again.

"Did you show the people in that bar Cora Steffani's

picture?" He smiled and I said hastily, "I mean, what did they say, when you did?"

"They can't be sure. Don't want to be sure." I could tell he was hesitating; there was something he could tell me. I just sat across the desk and stubbornly waited for him to do so. "We get what you might call rumors," he said. (I knew he was still trying to make up his mind about something else.) "This Jones may have been seen in Texas. May have been seen in Nevada."

"Does that help?"

"If he was in Texas, it was with a woman. In Nevada, they think he was alone."

"Who *was* Ed Jones?" I asked.

The Sergeant rubbed his chin. "You know Cora Steffani very well, I guess."

"Very well. For seventeen years."

"I'd like to show you something." He had made up his mind. He reached inside the desk. "More or less my own little idea," he said, "but a check is being made, just in case. I want you to look at this page and tell me what you see."

He had a brown imitation-leather book, a high school annual. He showed me a group picture, class of 1939. "Now, this"—he tapped a face in the back row —"is Edward Jones."

I looked at the glum, self-conscious young face. It only slightly resembled the rather horrible newspaper pictures of an older Ed Jones, in death. I'd never seen the face, alive, I knew. I glanced up at Sergeant Bartholomew. He was stubbornly just waiting. He wanted me to see something of my own accord.

So I looked back at the page and my eye ran through the ranks. All these lost, no longer existing faces, so young and so self-conscious, each so convinced that all the world was watching him. When I gasped, the Sergeant handed me a magnifying glass so quickly it was as if he had pulled it out of the air. The last girl in the first row was looking off haughtily to the right. She had Cora Steffani's nose.

She seemed to be a blonde. The chin was not too like, nor the brow. "That nose!" said I. And looked among the names and found, for the first time, and seared it into my memory, her name. Darlene Hite. "But that would be the *one!*" I cried. *"She* must have known Ed Jones. And it's Cora's nose, exactly! What are you doing about this?"

"Checking," said he.

"It hasn't been in the papers."

"A nose isn't a lot to go on. You have to stop and think, Miss Hudson. It's not our business to injure innocent people. Suppose this Hite girl was married and had a few kids and lived quietly someplace? The publicity in this thing is murder, you know. I'll tell you this, though. If you recognize that nose as easy and quick as you did, well, it sure must be like." I thought he seemed pleased.

"Do you know anything about this Darlene Hite?"

"Comes of a big family. Fifth child, two younger than she." (His grammar astonished me.) "No money. Darlene came to Hollywood and found some motion picture work." (People in and around Hollywood speak of "motion pictures" not "movies." Just as a pilot speaks of an "airplane" not a "plane.") "She lost out, I guess. She was working in a nightclub, up until last fall."

"Where is she now?"

He looked at me with a light in his eye. "She's missing," he said with a certain amount of satisfaction.

"Missing!"

"Dropped out of sight. Left the job. Said nothing to anybody. A misleading postal card is all the sign of her."

"Since last fall!"

"That's right."

"You *are* looking for her?"

"We sure are."

"Then, she's *not* married with kids and all that," I reproached him.

"She is not. We turned up that much so far. But still a nose in an old picture isn't much to go on and we don't know enough."

I seemed to have heard this before. "But it's so important," I cried. "Marcus is going to be crucified. The publicity will be murder for him. Wouldn't the newspapers, the public, help you find this Darlene Hite? Shouldn't you let them try?"

"It's a question, all right," said the Sergeant judiciously. "But if this Darlene Hite *is* the double who's been in on these stunts, then the general reading public isn't going to notice her around because she'll take care. Whereas, if Darlene Hite has nothing to do with it, then we should be able to locate her pretty soon and easily, without excitement. Follow me?"

"I guess so," I said reluctantly. "But . . ."

"Oh, we'll find her. It's not up to me to release her name and description but I can tell you this. If it seems

134

best, then they will be released." He was proud of his job and his colleagues, I could see.

"Are you asking me to keep quiet?"

He said, "I wouldn't have told you, Miss Hudson, if I hadn't thought you were a reasonable and balanced person. I don't expect you to go hysterically to some tabloid. I know you're pretty anxious, but we'll find her."

"How soon? It has to be soon. Could I make a long distance call on your telephone? I'll pay. I think . . . don't you? . . . we'd better know what's going on in Washington."

"I was wondering how I was going to find out," he said and shoved his phone over.

I called Marcus' very private number. Johnny Cunneen answered. "Where are you, Ollie? Charley's been having a fit."

"I'm in Los Angeles. How is Marcus?"

"Oh Lord, Ollie, it's a mess."

"Is it?" I wailed. "How?"

"Look, Ollie, I was *there* in the damn park. Not a soul spoke to Marcus or gave him a *thing*. There *was* no dame in any gray coat."

"But that's good. Isn't it?"

"Nobody believes me."

"What do you mean, nobody believes you? Why not?"

"Because I'm Marcus' boy, that's why. The idea is, I'd die for him. So naturally, I'd lie for him."

"*Who* doesn't believe you?"

"Ned Dancer, for one. He practically called me a liar."

"Is he *there?*"

"He got away," said Johnny in a voice of despair, "and all hell's going to break loose. . . . Wait. Here's Charley."

Charley Ives barked across the continent. "Ollie, for God's sake, where are you and why?"

"I'm in Los Angeles, finding things out. What's happening there?"

"That damned blue envelope—"

"Oh, no!"

"Oh, yes! Ned called the hospital back this morning and I, like a fool, let him do it."

"You had him there, at Marcus'?"

"We practically had him in chains. But listen. Cora, damn her eyes, told Doc Harper after we left, and she told Ned Dancer this morning, that she saw Marcus put the envelope inside the jacket of a book. Said it was a lurid-looking jacket and the title had the word 'Stranger' in it. I'll bet she deliberately saved that bit for Ned's ear, so I couldn't suppress anything. Well, of course, when Ned hung up he poked around on Marcus' shelves. How could I stop him? *And it was there.*"

"Oh, no," I moaned.

"Thriller *I'd* sent him in a big bundle, *two months ago.*"

"Oh, Charley . . . How *could* they?"

"Yeah, how could they? Those books were wrapped in our own shipping department. Thin little envelope, seemed to be stuck to the binding. Ned got it out. We may be able to prove it was glued. As if a little glue was enough to stop this thing." His voice faded.

"Did Marcus have that book with him?"

"In the park? Of course not."

"Then . . ."

"And how's he going to prove he didn't have it? Everybody thinks Johnny and Ruthie and all of them would lie for Marcus."

"Was the envelope bad, Charley?"

"Pretty bad," he said so quietly that my heart stopped. "We've got the envelope, but Dancer read the note. And what's worse, in the turmoil and confusion, he got away."

"How is Marcus?"

"The same," Charley's voice fell in descending tones of sorrow.

"Wait, Charley. Hang on, please." I repeated much of this rapidly to Sergeant Bartholomew. "I'm going to tell him about this Darlene Hite. I want you to agree. You see . . ." I began to flounder and bite my tongue. "There are . . . I mean, there must be . . . may be other kinds of police organizations that could help find her." He nodded. "She *has* to be found. Please, won't *you* tell him?"

Sergeant Bartholomew said briskly, "No. You go ahead, Miss Hudson. I'll want you to talk to my boss." So he left the room and I told Charley Ives about Darlene Hite.

I heard him sigh. "Teacher," he said much more cheerfully. "You revive me. I'll get Bud Gray on it. Of course, she may not be the right one."

"Of course," I repeated, "she may not be." But our hope pulsed on the wire, just the same, that she was.

"Let me talk to your policeman. Wait. What are you going to do now? Come back here, will you?"

"There?"

"Marcus would like to see you. I have an idea you can be useful."

137

"How?"

"I want you to help me get the truth out of the one we know has got it. The one we know where to find. It's got to be done, Ollie."

"Cora?" said I.

"How soon can you get a plane?"

"I don't know."

"Hurry. And don't go near Cora. Come here first." Charley's voice got sharp and stern. "Don't let her know that you're not still standing by. Maybe you don't like that, but it's damned necessary."

"I'll see you," I said, "probably by morning."

"Coz, you heard what I said?"

"I heard. I want to poke about L.A. a little more."

"Ollie," said he, "I hate to tell you this but the Los Angeles Police Department is on the telephone. I can even talk to them any time I want. You don't need to get their information by a personal interview, you know. Now come home, coz. All is forgiven."

"Charley, my boy," I said, nettled, "expect me when you see me."

I gave the phone to Sergeant Bartholomew, who had come back. Afterwards, he and his boss and I talked for an hour. (I never did pay for that phone call.) After that, the Sergeant and I went to the ratty little nightclub where Darlene Hite had been employed.

We found a girl singer and a man who played in the band, both of whom had known Darlene. For an experiment, I turned myself into Cora Steffani. I'm a pretty good mimic. I spoke in her affected voice and I lit a cigarette in her exaggerated way, with the eyes squinted against the smoke, with the wide flapping of the fingers to shake the match out, with the arm moving full length from the shoulder to flick ashes in a receptacle placed that far away. I not only used her flying gestures, I used what I knew of her inner attitude. I became alert for my own advantage, slightly mischievous, inquisitive, and full of schemes and yearnings. "Darlene Hite was about my size?" I asked. "Was she like me?" I let my hands plead, as Cora's do.

"Darlene had blond hair," the singer said. "What do you want to know all this for? I told you, she's in Vegas. I got a post card."

The Sergeant said quietly, "She's not in Vegas."

"Do I remind you of her?" I said in Cora's bursting manner.

"She isn't *anything* like you," the boy said distastefully.

I raised my brows and slid my eyes to the corners as Cora does.

"Darlene isn't so *nervous,*" he said. "She doesn't keep waving her arms around."

"Does she smoke?" asked the Sergeant.

"Yeah, but not like that. Darlene, she sticks a cigarette in her face and that's it. She don't make a big thing out of it." He stared at me with a kind of stolid disgust.

"She doesn't talk like that," the singer said. "Not so Eastern and fawncy. Darlene isn't trying to make herself so damn glamorous," she blurted. Evidently they didn't like me one bit.

"What's it about?" the boy glowered.

I changed. I let my hands fall and be heavy. I spoke a trifle nasally. "More like this?"

Now, they stared indeed. "What goes on?" the boy

said suspiciously. "Darlene's okay. Minds her business. I don't feel like answering questions."

"She works for a living," the singer said severely.

"I'm trying to find her, that's all," I said in my own voice. "Tell me anything you can about her. How does she walk? Does she turn her toes in or out? Has she any pet gesture?" I worked on it as I sometimes work on a characterization with my girls. I got them to say that Darlene walked, bent forward from the hips, and carried her head forward. That she smiled with her lips closed. But it was so slight. Almost nothing. The shadow of Darlene Hite against the mists of nothing was very thin.

Nor was there anything they could tell us about Darlene's departure. Nobody had come. No letter. No phone call had been noticed. Darlene had not said what her new job was or who had hired her. They despised us for not believing she was in Las Vegas.

I said to the Sergeant when we left, at last, "I may have overdone it, acting Cora Steffani. But was it just coincidence that they mentioned the hands, and the voice, and the business-like attitude?"

The Sergeant said, "It was very interesting, Miss Hudson." And our eyes met and both of us privately believed that Cora's traveling second body was Darlene Hite, all right. I've never seen a better demonstration of the difference between belief and knowledge.

Well, I went back on my tracks, hotel, airport. When I got on the plane for Chicago, one of my fellow passengers was Kent Shaw.

CHAPTER 13

When I got on the plane at 8:00 P.M. a late Los Angeles paper had the story, printed cautiously in a small box, full of hedges and alleges, about Marcus and Raymond Pankerman, *Dream Walker carries mystery message?* Ned Dancer had got away and the story was out and the fierce light was going to beat on Marcus and the jabber would begin and I felt sick.

Kent Shaw saluted me with appropriate surprise. He got out of his aisle seat and peered down the plane's length for two empties, side by side, assuming that we would so travel. But I quickly sat down in the aisle seat opposite his. I was tired, having had no real sleep in something like thirty-six hours, and I wasn't going to stay awake and talk if I could help it—not to hear his sour comments. I was feeling failure; time had run out. I wanted to be alone.

Just as soon as we were all buckled in and the door locked, Kent Shaw inclined his head. "What are you doing out here, Ollie? I thought you taught school nine days a week."

"Flying trip, obviously," said I. "Business."

His eyes were jumpy. He looked as tense and bouncy as usual, as if only the seat strap held him down. "What do you mean, business?" he demanded.

"My business," I said, making a big bright smile as rude as possible.

"Excuse me, I'm sure." He subsided with a grimace of his own. We lumbered in mysterious figure-eights over the field. After a while, Kent unfastened his belt and leaned over. "I see your friend, Cora, is at it again." He looked moist at the mouth, almost as if he licked his lips over this. "Notice, the paper?"

I felt revolted. He was to me a symbol of the pawing and fingering, the terrifying curiosity of millions. And I was exhausted, but he *would* talk. He was bursting with talk. "Excuse me, Kent," I said. "I've got to do my laundry."

"What?"

I fled to the tiny washroom where the roar and the rattle of flight is so loud. Conquering my sickness, pulling myself to numb but anyhow calmer acceptance, and taking what comfort I could from the homely chore, I washed out my collar and cuffs once more, while we bounced a little over the pass and streaked out above the desert land.

When at last I went back to my seat, Kent Shaw was humped over, apparently dozing. I softly asked for a pillow and a blanket and spread my laundry, nearly dry already, to hang over the edge of the seat-pocket before me. I went to sleep.

I've wondered. Did I save my life by doing my laundry? Would I have been enticed into telling Kent Shaw that I had heard of Darlene Hite? Would he then have thought I knew too much? I suppose not. After all, he couldn't get rid of the Los Angeles Police Department. And I didn't talk. I didn't tell him. But would he have taken fright, if I had? Did I save Cora's life, for then, by doing my laundry?

Now I can guess he was panting to know what I, so

close to Marcus, was thinking and doing. But he tried to seem, of course, less eager than he was.

Anyhow, stupid with sleep in Chicago, I changed planes for Washington, and since Kent Shaw stayed on for New York, I got away. I had no paraphernalia. It was only a matter of slipping on my coat and walking out with the leg-stretchers. If Kent Shaw had been working at some cautious way to pump me between Chicago and New York, he was disappointed.

The morning paper had a bigger, juicier story. Oh, it was out and it would soon be roaring.

Marcus was just the same, just the same. I hadn't wired. I took a cab to his house. Charley Ives grabbed me with both hands and smacked my cheek. "What, no suitcase? Come in, coz. There's a council of war." He was kind, but I suddenly felt very feeble. What had I been doing that was any good?

Marcus has a room full of books and papers, deep in the house, and there I found him and embraced him and he was just the same. Not a man who bewails cruel fate or cries, Oh, why have they done this to me! He looked his usual blend of spryness and serenity. And if he was hurt in his feelings he didn't bother to express it. "Well, Ollie, I hear you've done some detective work, too."

"Not much, Uncle John." I looked around.

Bud Gray was there, calm and alert. Johnny Cunneen was there, miserably angry. Little Ruthie Miller's nose was pink with woe. Sig Rudolf was there. (He is a lawyer and an in-law.) His broad face, and even his scalp where the hair recedes, was mottled red-and-white, as if his effort to suppress distress and rage were only skin deep. Charley Ives, however, looked easier than I had last seen him. He'd been in action. He and Bud Gray were men of action. They understood fighting, and the waiting involved, too, and all sorts of real things. I could feel I was in the presence of professionals.

As I told them all I knew, I could see that over and above what a real detective had discovered, it was scarcely anything. I don't think they were impressed by my wispy bits of description. All of that seemed feeble and feminine and fairly useless.

They began to tell me what they knew. They had already dug up three people who had been in the park at half past two, day before yesterday, on the 5th of May. Who all admitted they had watched Marcus, he being a celebrity. Two of them had seen no one approach him. The third one said he had seen a woman in a gray coat speak to Marcus and hand him a piece of paper.

"He did not," Gray said. "He's the kind of witness who doesn't even know he is lying. Remembers, to suit what he thinks the facts are."

Charley said, *"He's* talked to reporters, already. *He'd* be the one."

"Oh, there'll be more such witnesses," Gray said. "Some of them will have seen it all in a dream."

Johnny Cunneen said, "I was on the next bench, keeping an eye out, as I always do. But me they don't listen to." He held his head.

"Pankerman admits to being in the park," Charley said to me, "and all three witnesses say they saw *him*. We don't doubt he was there."

"Did you see him, Uncle John?"

"Neither Johnny nor I saw him," said Marcus. "I suppose he kept around that corner, behind the trees."

"Does Raymond Pankerman admit he asked that favor of a strange woman? Does he admit he gave her an envelope?"

"Oh no. No, indeed. Not at all. For the rest, he stands just as he said he would, on the Fifth Amendment." Gray looked disgusted.

"So as not to incriminate himself," Charley said. "And that's devilish. Because he does incriminate himself, and Marcus, too."

"He has been behind this entire sequence," Marcus said.

"Pankerman!" I was astonished.

"Of course." Charley ticked off points. "In the park at the right moment. Lying, by this damned device of keeping suspiciously still. His name, his handwriting on the note in the blue envelope. Of course, he's behind it."

"Why?"

Then Marcus told me how his own hunch had been Pankerman's fall.

"Just for *revenge?*" cried I. "Why, that's . . . that's . . ." I had no words for what I thought it was. Personal revenge seemed pitifully small and out of place against the scale of this affair. Personal revenge has been almost outlawed by doctrines of "adjustment" and self-analysis. The whole battery of popular psychology is trained in the opposite direction. Even violence, even war, is no longer thought of as revenge. But it *is,* I thought. Revenge is *exactly* what heats the blood. We *want* revenge. We *want* to punish. Oh Lord, I thought, who can be wise? What human being —when his blood, his glands, the motivations of his energies are so designed? I knew Marcus would say, as

145

Dr. Barron would say: Anger is ours, built in our blood, to move our bodies. We can't deny it. It's just that our brains must tell us what shall make us angry.

"What was in the envelope?" I asked. God knows *I* was angry.

"It's locked up," said Charley, "with a couple of handwriting experts. Purports to be a wind-up, in Pankerman's handwriting (and I'll bet that's genuine, myself), of some secret and damnable dealings between him and Marcus. Winding up, because Pankerman is going to be incapacitated. There's enough implied, and just enough, to be damned cleverly convincing."

"Convincing?"

"Some people are going to think I am a traitor," Marcus said and I, thinking of all the stainless years behind him, thought my heart would break.

"No, they won't," I cried. "We'll stop it. How did they get the envelope into the book? Charley, you should know that."

Charley said, "I've had our place turned upside down. It would have been too easy. Anybody, dropping around, could have wandered into the shipping department. Anybody with the slightest cover of a reason to see me, for instance, or any one of the editors. Or it could have been a boy friend of a clerk. Even a fake inspector of some kind. *When* it was done, we can roughly guess because we know the shipping date. March 10th. But I send Marcus books every month. Not hard to know."

"The envelope was glued in?"

"We think it was. They didn't want it to fall out, of course. But it was done by gluing a corner of the

146

gummed strip on the envelope itself and who can prove it didn't *happen* to fold out, *happen* to stick?"

I was silent, appalled.

"Pankerman is in it and Cora Steffani is in it, and this Darlene Hite is very possibly the other woman."

"I'm sure she is," I said.

"And the whole thing," said Charley Ives, "has been working up to this."

Ruthie Miller, with her tiny hands clenched said, "They are just fiends!" I saw Marcus smile at her.

"I can see, vaguely," I said, "why Pankerman might do it. I suppose he had to use Darlene or somebody else who looks as much like Cora. What I don't understand—why would Cora Steffani want to hurt Marcus? Or . . . or you, Charley? Or . . ." I floundered, "or *me,* for that matter? She knows how we feel about Marcus. Is she doing this to me and to you, just for the notoriety?"

Charley said impatiently, "Teacher, she *is* doing it."

"But I thought you and she were . . . almost together again. I know you're fond of her. You *like* a rascal. I understand that. And I've rather liked her myself. What motive overpowers that . . . well, call it fondness?"

Charley looked at me with pity. Gray said, "Guessing why isn't going to help us find this Darlene Hite. Which is what we've got to do. An awful lot of people are looking for her, right now. But if she killed that man in L.A., believe me, she could be out of the country."

"I wonder," said Marcus. We all listened. "Tell me," said the old gentleman, "if these people worked out this plan, as they must have done, far in advance

147

and in great detail, could such a plan include this killing?"

"No," I said. "Of course not. Ed Jones happened to recognize the other woman in Chicago. So they had to keep him quiet. Of course, they couldn't have planned on killing him from the beginning. I don't think even Cora—" I stopped. (Why *even* Cora? Did I think Cora was blood-driven, then? Cora would take revenge? For what?)

"How did this woman, Cora, *know* he'd be dead in the ferns on March 28th?" asked Marcus.

"Perhaps she didn't," I said. "She *was* shocked. I remember. Don't you, Charley?"

"She expected something dead," Charley reminded me. "But I agree. I don't think she expected it to be human."

"Then," said Marcus, pursuing his own lucid line of reasoning, "there was a change in plan, and the question is, how were these two women in communication?"

"A change, sir?"

"Isn't it too much to suppose that they had for many weeks planned for something to be dead in those ferns so that when it became necessary to kill a man, he fitted right in?"

"Ned Dancer had the switchboard operator bribed and Mildred Garrick was paying the maid," Charley said, surprising me, "and Ollie was there, all along. Kept there no doubt to observe that there *was* no communication."

"I observed none," I said unhappily.

Marcus gave me a swift loving look. "But they changed a plan. They did communicate. Now, I would

148

like to suppose there had been no Ed Jones. What was the original plan, before they changed it?"

"Oh, I suppose more stuff," said Charley. "A few more well-known people, until they had drawn enough attention."

"Would it have been quite so violently publicized," said Marcus, "without that dead man?"

"I see what you mean, sir," said Charley. "That dead body is the one thing that really put this show on the road. But that was an afterthought. A revision."

"Yes. So I wonder," said Marcus, "if they had been left with the original scheme only, would they not be planning yet another of these . . . occurrences. A capper incident, to sandwich me in the middle and help the excitement along?"

We considered this. It seemed *right* to me. A deliberate anticlimax. A good showman faking a show not to look like a show, might do that.

"They don't need it now," Gray said.

"But when you suggested that Darlene Hite has left the country," Marcus turned to him, "I began to wonder if her job is quite over. Somebody very clever has designed this thing."

"How in the name of heaven," cried Johnny Cunneen, leaving off worrying his fingernails with his teeth, "can you *guess* what they'll do, if they *are* planning another one? It may be anywhere in the whole country. It can happen to any one of thousands of people. It lasts about five minutes. You can't set any trap."

Charley said, "But if you could, Darlene Hite would walk right into it."

149

Gray shook his head. "She's too smart," he said didactically.

"Just the same," said Charley, "on a bare chance, I think we'll try to be ready."

"How can you?" cried Ruthie.

"Have a plane set to go. Do that much. It only costs money. First sign of any trance, we can take off, and with luck . . . After all, this Hite woman does not really vanish into thin air."

"She does about as well," said Gray.

Charley looked stubborn. Sig Rudolf cleared his throat. He was about to say something ponderous. But I said, "Charley, my boy, I hate to tell you this. But wherever Cora may walk in a dream, there'll be folks, and if folks, then probably a telephone. We're not getting anywhere. We can't just wait and hope Cora does it again and chase around in airplanes . . ." (which was absurd for air-worn me to be saying). "That's so feeble," I sputtered. "While Marcus is going to be hurt." (*Is* being hurt, I thought.) "What *are* the reactions?"

"Grim faces," Gray told me, "around the Capitol."

"Everybody knows," said Charley, and now he was up and walking around, "that Marcus is no liar. But, damn it, the thing has got to be explained."

"But we *can* explain it, can't we?" Ruthie said. "It's just a plot against him."

"Baby," said Charley Ives, "we have to explain with bells on. We have to do it down to the last hook and eye. We got to get confessions and tape recordings and cross-examinations and witnesses and breakdowns and the works."

Sig Rudolf said, "Certainly. Then you can sue, and

150

get it into the courts, where there is some orderly machinery. In centuries of struggle, we've figured out the best way men know yet to get at the truth, expose the guilty, protect the innocent, and if we now by-pass the work of these centuries and accuse and convict and sentence a man by gossip and rumor—"

"Sig," said Charley patiently. *"We know.* Unfortunately, there's no law that I ever heard about which says a woman *mustn't* be in two places at once, if she can manage to do the trick. We can hardly drag Cora into court for that. Let's get on, shall we? Now that Ollie's back."

"Tell me what I can do?" I said.

"Pankerman is sitting behind a mass of lawyers, three deep. Darlene Hite is not available. But Cora Steffani is in that hospital where I was smart enough to put her and keep her handy. So Cora Steffani is our bird-in-hand, and she has got to be broken down until she tells us. Now, you, Ollie, are going to stand by Cora for auld lang syne . . ." I began to shake my head. "Even the lie about Marcus," continued Charley, "while it upsets you, still can't wean you from your high principles. Can it? You have no proof that Marcus didn't do it. You don't believe in condemning people."

"No," I cried. "No."

"Ollie, you're going to have to."

"I *can't* pretend to be that stupid," I flared. "Cora's not that gullible. She knows what I think of Marcus. The whole world knows."

"Loyalties," said Charley, "conflict. Yeah. Well, somehow or other, you've got to keep on being her only friend. I don't care how you handle it."

"How can I pretend to be her friend when she's lying about Marcus? There's a limit to what's plausible."

"I'm telling you what you can do to help," he said. (Charley Ives and I were going to fight.) "You asked me. Act, why don't you? Use your Art."

"You don't even understand what it *is*," I cried.

"Make-believe, isn't it?" he snapped. "How have you managed to stick around being loyal to her since Ed Jones died? Keep *that* up."

(I couldn't imagine how I'd managed. I didn't know.) "I was wrong," I cried. "Absolutely stupid and wrong. But what I'm trying to tell you, for me to step out of character . . ."

"Just be yourself, Teacher," said Charley. "Just be a kind of unshakable saint, sweetly naïve, nobly aloof, devoted to principle, and stubborn as an ornery old country mule."

"Charley, my boy," I began, "your childish ideas—"

"Shut up, coz, and listen to me. You've got to be tolerant and kind and loyal and understanding."

"Who says so!" I raged. "And what are *you* going to be?"

"Me, I'm going to be so un-nice and caddish and ungentlemanly," said Charley Ives, "that you and she will quite agree. I'll rile her up. She'll turn to you."

"You're a dreamer," I said. "She'll never confess to *me*. Charley, you're a fool!" I was so mad at Charley Ives that I'd forgotten there were other people in the room.

Bud Gray said, calmly, "It's an old police trick,

Miss Hudson. The mean cop and the mild sympathetic one, working in a pair."

"I'm to be a policeman, then?"

Marcus said placidly, "You're not a bad actress, Ollie. You're a pretty good one."

I looked at him and the wind blew wider. "Of course, I'll try," I said. "*Anything,* Uncle John. If you think it might work."

"I imagine," said Marcus, "Charley can make her pretty mad if he wants to."

"I don't doubt *that,*" I said. "It's just—"

"It's the only . . ." Charley put his hands in his pockets as if to keep himself from shaking me. "What can we do but try to upset her and trip her up? She's safe with her mouth shut, so far, and she knows that and all the or-elseing in the world isn't going to make her forget that. But if she gets good and mad at me, I should think she might blurt out something to a female chum." He looked me in the eye. "Yes, it's dirty."

"I don't *care* how dirty it is," I cried. "That doesn't worry me. I'm touched by your little character sketch, Charley, my boy, and your faith and all. But I don't think it will work. You never have understood how it is between Cora and me."

"Likewise, I'm sure," he snapped. "And it's got to work. Come on, let's get going. Try doing what I say." Charley looked dangerous.

"Yes, sir," I said, as humbly as I could which wasn't very. He threw my coat around me. Sig begged a ride in the plane Charley had waiting. Gray was coming, too. We said good-by to Marcus. Good-by and good hope.

153

CHAPTER 14

Charley and Bud Gray sat together and talked while I, beside Sig Rudolf, listened and did not always hear his oratorical fuming. We would be in New York soon after noon, although I'd almost stopped noticing the days go around.

The papers were sniffing at the story, now, much more boldly. By nightfall, they would be in full cry. Whoever believed that Marcus would not lie would be wearing graver faces as the uproar increased, ink spilled, tongues wagged. We could deny, deny . . . deny. We could tell all the truth we knew until our faces were blue, and it wouldn't be enough. It couldn't still the voices or stop the ink flowing.

Charley Ives was right. We had to have a fully detailed explanation on our side.

We were nearly in when Charley came over. "Where will you tell Cora you've been?" he asked me crisply. "Better decide."

"Denver, Los Angeles, Washington."

"Why not just Washington, for two nights and a day. You can't explain Los Angeles." His voice became rather gentle. "Ollie, don't you understand? You're going to have to be lying to her."

"I presume," I said stonily, "that when you lie you should try not to get caught at it. Kent Shaw was on the plane out of Los Angeles. Who knows if he's seen her, or seen someone who's told her?"

"I beg your pardon," Charley said. "Kent Shaw have anything to offer?"

"If he did, I didn't take it. I went to sleep."

"You must be tired." He was being cautious and gentle. "It was good of you to go."

"Not much good," I said. I don't like kid gloves.

"Ollie, let's not fight."

"Charley, my boy," I said wearily, "the opposite of fighting isn't, I hope, buttering each other up with patronizing praise. I realize that I am the rankest amateur at this police business, although I must say you're not very good at acting, either. Don't worry about me. I'll try to do as you suggest."

Charley's face was pink. "Sometimes, I can't understand how you can make such thoroughly nasty remarks, while looking as if you were after the Holy Grail," he said. "You scare the life out of me."

"Why?"

"If I didn't know you were a petty thief, I'd be telling myself you *could not* tell a lie."

"Thief!" I squealed.

"Well," he said, cocking a blue eye, "it was more or less my property."

"What was?"

"At least I didn't steal it from you. I stole it from somebody else."

"Charley," I bounced upright, "you are the most exasperating . . . !"

155

"Well," he said, blotting my sentence and my whole train of thought out, with his sudden deep sadness, "put up with me, Ollie. Let's put up with each other, shall we? For Marcus' sake?"

I was shocked. "There must be some misunderstanding," I murmured.

"I think so," he said. "And I'm a better *actor* than you think. Never mind. Lie your head off, to Cora, will you, coz?"

"It'll be lying," I said. "It won't be Art, though."

"Do you think," he said through his teeth, *"you're* not exasperating? That fight's thirteen years old."

"Truce. Truce," I said. "I'll be her only friend, the best I can. It's a lousy role, Charley." Tears started in my eyes.

"Aw, Teacher," said Charley softly and touched my hair lightly.

I shivered violently. I couldn't, thereafter, move or look. In another moment, I knew he had gone back to talk with Gray.

I streaked uptown to my apartment and peeled off that detestable blue taffeta dress. My rooms looked like an archeological exhibit, and all my things were relics of a former era.

I hurried out of there to the hospital. I could not . . . could not solidly imagine my role. It was unprepared, undigested, unrehearsed. I knew I was stepping on stage to do what I warned my girls never to do. I was not secure in the part. I didn't understand the woman I was about to present.

Charley was there already. Downstairs, he pounced

on me. Bud Gray, he told me, was already hidden in the room next to Cora's, with some listening device against her wall.

"Go first," said Charley. "Establish yourself."

I sighed. "I'll have to try it my own way," I warned him.

"Any way that does it." He was all policeman.

So I went upstairs and tapped on her door.

Cora was wearing a gold-colored robe of silk, embroidered with black dragons. She was sitting in an easy chair, talking to a strange young man. "Why, Ollie! Where have you been!" she exclaimed. But she was more wary than cordial. She knew she had offended me beyond all forgiveness. How could I make her believe otherwise?

"You'd hardly believe where I've been," I said grumpily.

She introduced the young and rather pink-cheeked man as a henchman of Mildred Garrick's. "Press?" said I. "Oh me . . ."

"In a friendly way, Miss Hudson," the young man said. "Message from Mildred, that's all."

I went over to the high bed and lay myself up upon it. "I'm exhausted," I said. "Go on with whatever it is."

"It's nothing," said Cora. "Mildred sends this young snoop around from time to time. Mildred's been . . . kind." (Mildred had been making the most of her inside track.) Cora got up and swished about, the long folds of golden silk boiling about her quick feet. "Ollie, where *have* you been? I thought you'd gone forever."

"I've been detecting," I said.

"Oh?" Cora lit a cigarette in her exaggerated way.

"Where have I not been?" said I. "I've been to Denver, Los Angeles, Washington."

"Since day before yesterday?" she cried prettily. Maybe she hid alarm.

"What's the news?" said the little boy from the newspaper.

"No news." I closed my eyes.

"Then what are you here for?" asked my old friend, Cora. Her voice was ready for weeping or for rage, whichever way the cat would jump. (I was the cat.) "I suppose you want a piece of my scalp," she challenged.

I said, "No."

"No?"

I opened my eyes. "Cora," (I suppose I had on what Charley Ives would call my Holy Grail look) "swear to me that you don't understand this thing. You only know you dream."

Cora looked queer. "Ollie, I swear." Her voice trembled very nicely.

"Two impossible things before breakfast," I misquoted. "Either you are a wicked liar. Or you have strange dreams. Choose one, I suppose."

"Miss Hudson," said the pink-faced lad, excitedly. "You think John Paul Marcus *may* be mixed up with Pankerman and that crowd?"

"No, no, no," I said quickly. "I wonder if Pankerman isn't *using* Cora's dream."

"Hey, that's an idea!" he cried. It wasn't much of an idea. "But . . ." he looked around at Cora in apology, "you do," he said to me, "believe she dreams?"

158

"What else can I think?" I said. "She might want publicity. She might want notoriety. But to get it by wrecking Marcus . . . I cannot believe she'd do a thing like that to"—I let a beat go by—"people she loves."

Cora chose tears, of course. "Ollie, darling, how can I tell you? I was afraid I'd lost you. Nobody . . . nobody else knows what all this does to me." She was all broken up. "I should have known," she quavered sentimentally, "that *you'd* be fair. You've always been the fairest person I've ever known."

The pink boy went away, all agog.

The moment he was gone, Cora said, suspending her tears, "But I don't know whether to believe you . . ."

"Don't then," I said. There would be no more tears. We never had been sentimental.

"Why did you tear off all over the country?" she demanded.

"I wanted to know. Talked to Jo Crain, Monti, Dr. Barron."

"Isn't he a lamb?" she cried, falsely. (Put-on, I thought.)

"And people in Los Angeles," I told her.

"Davenport?"

"No. Bartholomew. Police."

"Well?"

I shrugged and threw my hands out. "You just are not that clever," I said and the line rang true. Her eyes flickered. "So I don't know what it is," I continued, "and since you swear to me . . ."

She swished herself around and sat down. "Don't

gimlet-eye me, Ollie. There's no way to understand it. I'm sick of trying. *We* don't need to talk about it, do we?"

Silence.

"What are you going to do?" I asked after a while.

"Go abroad, maybe. Run away."

"No vaudeville turns? No Confessions?"

"I've had offers."

"I'm glad you're not taking them."

"Bad enough, as it is," she said, playing forlorn.

"Cora, can't the doctors help you?"

"They don't seem to." She accepted this implication quickly. "And I am so tired of this cage. Do you know how long I've been in this hospital? I can't leave it. I feel as if I wouldn't get across the street with my limbs still on."

"No more would you," said I.

Cora sighed deeply. "It's good to have you back. I've been lonely." She looked sideways. "Where is Charley Ives? Do you know?"

I didn't have to produce an answer because Charley Ives was rapping on the door. He came in and the walls bulged. I guessed he'd been next door and had heard much that had been said. I pulled at my skirt and sat up more primly and somewhat defensively.

"Ah, girls," said Charley. "Letting your hair down?" He looked at me as if he'd like to throttle me.

Cora's lids fluttered. Otherwise she was motionless.

"You," said Charley to her with no more preliminaries, "are a liar and a louse. And you," he said to me, "are a fool."

160

"Well!" said Cora brightly. "This is charming. Do go on."

"Do you think I won't?" Charley put his hands in his pockets. "Cousin Ollie sees no evil. But I never did wear rose-colored glasses. It's Pankerman's money that pays for this prank."

"It doesn't cost anything," said Cora plaintively.

"It will. You're implicated up to your neck in slander and fraud and homicide."

"Am I?" She looked sideways at him. "Why aren't I in jail, then? Wouldn't they have to prove all this, Charley dear?"

"Ah," he said easily, "Darlene Hite can prove it."

Cora was good. Very good. She didn't startle. She was braced, of course. She'd been ready for thunder and lightning from Charley Ives. She didn't even make the mistake of saying, "Who is Darlene Hite?" She said nothing.

I said it. "Who is Darlene Hite?"

"The other one," Charley answered. "The astral body. A real woman with Cora's nose."

"Somebody wants to get in the act," said Cora with superb ennui.

"You're not ill," said Charley. "I'll pay no more bills here. Why should I keep you?" She narrowed her eyes. "Besides," he continued, "since you and Darlene Hite together killed a man, your next stop is jail."

"How could I kill anybody in a dream?" she said mournfully. "Who's this Darlene? Somebody wants her name in the papers, too? What a name! Why don't you bring this Darlene? Before you make corny threats, Charley, dear."

"I'll bring her."

"When?"

"When I'm ready." But Charley just wasn't convincing.

Cora laughed. "Trying to save your precious Grandpa?" she mocked. "What did you do? Hire somebody? Are you blaming yourself, Charley, dear?" Now her voice was pure poison. She enjoyed it. "Are you thinking that if only you and I were still married, why, I'd have cut my tongue out, wouldn't I?"

"You'll wish you had," he said, and it looked to me as if he was the one who was going to be enraged.

Cora said, "Oh, Charley, go away. Leave us. Make him go, Ollie." Then, pitifully, "I can't take much more." But she could. She was enjoying it.

Charley said, "I'll tell you what you couldn't take. A man having the guts to say he didn't want you." Muscles tightened in her neck. In mine, too. "Fell for each other, in a big way, didn't we?" Charley said. "All of our dreams came true. Only trouble was, I wasn't quite so deep asleep, and I proceeded to wake up. And had the nerve to say so. Being unwilling to spend the rest of my life in hell, for one mistake. And we had pious speeches, didn't we? About being good friends. And oh, we were so gay. And lust," said Charley Ives, "for a dirty indirect revenge in your filthy little heart."

Cora was getting angry, now, all right.

"Did you think," said Charley, "that I, who'd had my eyes opened years ago, wouldn't *know*? You're so small you'd get into a scheme like this, just for your name in the papers. But it's peachy-keen, it's jolly fun, isn't it? . . . to ruin John Paul Marcus, while you're at it, for the oldest cliché in the book. The woman scorned."

"You may go," said Cora loftily.

"When you turned on the—shall I say?—full personality," said Charley and oh, he was insulting, "even then I wouldn't stay married. And you had to play civilized—"

"Get out," said Cora in a voice that was thick and ugly.

Then Charley was calm and smiling. "Poor . . . cheap . . . mean . . . little thing . . ." he drawled. He left us and closed the door softly.

He'd done his share. She looked as if she'd explode. Now it was for me to catch her reaction. To receive the indiscretions born of this rage. But I, I was so absolutely flabbergasted at Charley's tactics that I could hardly pull myself together. I didn't know the role. It was impossible. "Why . . . the . . . conceited . . . ass!" I muttered. It wasn't good. It was dreadfully bad. Put-on, as Dr. Barron would say.

Cora turned around. "Get out," she screamed at me. "Get out, Ollie, darling darling Cousin Ollie. Get out, Teacher!"

I slipped off that high bed. "I shouldn't have heard. I can forget."

"In a pig's eye you'll ever forget," she screeched. "It's water on the desert to you. Think I don't know? You're mad about Charley Ives. You're crazy for him, yourself!"

So I took up my bag. "Call me, if you like," I said as quietly and stolidly as I could. "When you are feeling better. And don't worry about the bills," I said over my shoulder. "I'll stop at the desk and take care of them."

Cora said chokingly, "Just let me alone, you and your noble charity."

"Oh, I will," I said, "whatever you say." (But I tried once more.) "I haven't anything to do," I said, "since I've lost my job, standing by you."

She screamed at me, "Get out!"

So I left her.

Charley Ives met me at the elevator and we rode down silently. In the lobby he said to me, "I was wrong, Teacher. And you were right." He said it straightforwardly with his blue eyes steady.

I wanted to look everywhere but at his face. But I said to his unhappy eyes, "Maybe she'll call me. I think she may."

"Do you?" he said respectfully.

"Because she can use me," I said. "She has, already."

"How, Ollie?"

"Olivia Hudson, Marcus' kin, on the wrong side. And that boy gone running to tell what he heard." Charley winced. "It doesn't matter," I said. "Marcus knows."

Then Bud Gray joined us.

"Anything?" asked Charley.

"Not a sound. Doesn't talk to herself, apparently. Good try." Both of them were sober in defeat.

"What can we do now?" I asked nervously.

"Find Darlene Hite, I guess," said Charley. "Shall I take you home, Ollie?" He was sober and sad and all the thunder and lightning was gone.

"I better go up to school and resign."

"Must you?" Charley was troubled.

"It's a part of the act, I think." I took pity on him. "Now, Charley, my boy, don't look so distressed. You were about as nasty as anyone could possibly be."

His eye sparked. "Thank you," he said.

"That Cora," said Gray, "sure wasn't having any comfort from you, Ollie."

"She had to scream," I said, "and accuse *somebody* of *something*. Oh, I suppose I irritate her a thousand ways. It's not as if we were together or alike, you know. We began together but we went different ways. We still check each other as if we were each other's measuring-sticks. Hard to explain." I stopped mumbling. "I'm not excusing that terrible performance. I was bad."

Gray said, as so many people will, "You did your best."

But Charley said, "If she had, she'd know it."

I wanted to bawl. But I said, "They do say them as can, do. And them as can't, teach. Don't they? Sorry I muffed it." So I got away.

CHAPTER 15

I was permitted to resign without protest. I think I would have been discharged, anyway. Miss Reynolds couldn't understand my position, of course, and even if she had, there was just too much publicity.

Cora did use me. The news went around that I refused to call her a liar. Which implied, no matter how you twisted it or turned it, that I (of all people) thought Marcus might be the one who was lying. So Marcus was being hurt and I was helping. Although my bit was hardly significant in the flood.

Questions were asked in official places. Usually reliable sources and unidentified spokesmen hedged and hinted. Politicians puffed up with loud cries that the people be told. They didn't say what. Committees were rumored. Columnists recapitulated and among them there were the "objective analyzers," the angry partisans, staunch defenders, witty scoffers, and sad reluctant viewers with alarm. Everywhere, the eye met the printed suggestion that there must be more than met the eye.

It *was* released, on our side, that there existed a Darlene Hite, and now the entire nation was looking for her. That high school annual picture and a theatrical photographer's highly retouched version of her grown-up face were printed everywhere, side by side with Cora's. Nobody found her.

Charley Ives went to Washington the following Monday. Bud Gray stood by in New York. There was a plane ready. A forlorn hope.

Cora stayed, secluded and protected, in that hospital. I paid the bills (a fact that got out and hurt Marcus, too). She kept to her story. What else was she to do? She was safe as long as she did. She could read. She knew from the newspapers how we had heard of Darlene Hite. She also knew we couldn't find her.

Raymond Pankerman (although he was in the toils, personally) must have been gratified. Marcus was being hurt.

As for Kent Shaw, he was seen in his usual haunts and he joined, naturally enough, in the endless discussions. But we gave him no thought. Why should we?

Happy little man. Swelling to the point of madness, scurrying shabbily about, with the great secret of his masterpiece, his swan-song, bathing his veins with joyous self-congratulations. Reading and listening and swelling, swelling with that poisonous pride!

I was right. Cora did call me. The mere existence of a Darlene Hite, acquainted with Ed Jones, had done us some good. At least, it was fuel for theories on our side. So maybe Cora felt she needed to flaunt me. Maybe she was thinking of those bills. Anyhow, she called me, on Monday, and I went.

She made an apology. Said she'd been upset.

I, groping for my part, said that Charley obviously had been trying to upset her. And Charley had been nasty.

"I loathe him," said Cora.

"Naturally," I said.

Cora looked at me oddly. "But Charley's psychology wasn't bad," she said airily. "If a woman did want a man she couldn't have, she'd protect herself."

"How do you mean?" said I.

"Why, she'd cover it up. She'd seem to . . . dislike him. Don't you think so, Ollie?"

I shrugged for an answer, while Cora watched and licked her lip. Then, in mutual relief, we left that subject. It almost seemed that we were back in the old arrangement. We were as we had been, old acquaintances, neither of us altogether fond or trusting, but still each other's habits, and able to stay in the same room, part hostile, part resigned.

So I was there when Kent Shaw turned up, to call. (Perhaps he took care to see that someone should be. It was no time for him to be seeing Cora alone.) He came glumly, that afternoon, and hadn't much to say. It was, I thought, a concession to pure curiosity, which he resented in himself. This is what he did say. "Cora, dear, why don't you go to Spain? Or Rome? Very pleasant in Spain. And Rome is charming."

"I very well may," she told him.

"Book passage, then," he urged. "Ten days ahead, at least."

Cora said somewhat impatiently, "I know."

"Doesn't cost too much and well worth it to get away. You can afford it, can't you?"

"I expect so," she murmured.

"Tell me when to send the usual basket of fruit." Kent rose to go.

Cora grimaced. "Oranges? Dates?"

"No lemons, dear," Kent said. (This seemed to me to be somewhat inane.)

"Sugared fruit, Kent darling," Cora said, "if you really want to please me."

"Of course," Kent said, "we want to please you. Don't we, Ollie?" And Kent went away.

I thought it was feeble persiflage, chatter, nothing. What they were really saying to each other, I didn't hear. I can hear it now.

He: It will be over soon.

She: Yes.

He: Ten days from now.

She: I know. I remember.

He: Then you will be rewarded.

She: I expect to be.

He: I expect to pay.

She: I know the date.

He: Don't fail. No lemons wanted.

She: Just be ready with the sugar, the money.

He agreed. And I sat by, her old friend who knew her well, and asked her when he had gone, if she really thought of leaving the country. She said she had really thought of it. She said she was weary of all the public uproar. It occurred to me to wonder how she could afford it. But that was all.

So time dragged on, ten more days of it. And it was a dreadful time. Hard-headed investigators, of course, took no stock in the supernatural. But they could not find Darlene although hundreds of women with noses anything like Cora's had been crucified for a day. And now the gags began. Wise-crackers called Darlene Hite a white herring. Marcus was being red-washed, some said. And this frothy stuff hurt him and cheapened him, and broke my heart.

Worse, of course. The envelope had been in Marcus' house, and none could explain who had put it there or how. Unless it had been handed to Marcus in the park, where Raymond Pankerman had been, at the right time. No one could explain how, if Pankerman was behind it all, how . . . how . . . how could Cora Steffani in New York know what she had known.

. . . What Dr. Barron would say on a given afternoon in Colorado . . . The look of the book that Marcus owned . . . and always the dead man in the ferns . . . that hardy haunt would rise.

Even so, I didn't know how bad it was for Marcus, until the day Charley Ives came back, the 20th of May, and met me in the little snack bar at the hospital.

If Marcus went to the park, Charley told me, knots of people tended to gather. They would keep their distance but they stared without pleasure, uneasy, doubtful, hideously curious. That was the public. Marcus no longer went, every day, to the park.

What was happening to him privately, Charley said, was hard to define, impossible to prevent. A thing as uncapturable as a breeze. The withdrawing of respect and confidence. Softly, without proclamation, people withdrew. They did not cry angry disillusion or even cut him dead. But it was not the same, any more. Secrets were not spilled out to him in perfect flow. Problems were not opened before him, pro and con, in full detail. His advice was not asked for. His store of wisdom and experience was not drawn upon, but rested, unused, unregarded. Charley said it was a spiritual punishment that could kill a man. So Marcus read a lot, kept by himself. Those of his household, Charley said, were in an agony of surface cheer and helpless grief.

Well (although because I am so much smaller, it only happened to me in a smaller way), I knew what it was. From me, also, people drew away. They did not understand me. (At the hospital so much, with this freak of a woman. Did I *believe* in her supernatural powers? An educated modern person like me? Or did I *know* something?) They shunned me for an unknown quantity, or despised me for a traitor to Marcus. Washed their clean hands of someone so freakish and incomprehensible. Oh, I felt it. It hurts. How precious a thing it is to meet everywhere an assumption that you are most probably decent and normally intelligent. If this is lost, you are left in the loneliest kind of place, a world without any fellows where you find no peers and don't belong.

Charley himself was clearly in anguish over Marcus. He said he wished he could figure out how to put Cora over some kind of rack, and wring the truth out of her. But he said ruefully that racks don't wring truth, unfortunately.

I said regretfully that I, in my part, wasn't getting anywhere. I said she used me gladly, even cynically. But she would never confide in me.

171

"Just the same," he said, "try to hang on and stick to it, coz. May help us yet. We never know what'll help."

"Oh, I agree," I said. "And nothing matters now but to help Marcus."

He looked at me with a tiny curl of the old teasing light in his eye. "What, nothing?" said he.

"Nothing at all," said I.

And I thought to myself, someday, somehow, I may find the role for me, the one I can play-act for Cora Steffani that will strike close to the bone and shake her heart and upset her defenses. I will find the rack on which to stretch her.

Bud Gray came in. We looked at him hopefully.

"That Darlene," he said, gloomily, climbing on a stool at my other side. "She's the clever one. I sure could use a dame who knows how to get invisible the way she does."

"What would you do with her?" I asked idly.

"Use her in my business. Have her steal the papers . . . out of the black portfolios of the bearded strangers," said Bud in bitter jest. "And then vanish."

"Charley, my boy," I said suddenly, "speaking of stealing, what on earth did you think I ever stole from you?"

"Photograph," he said absently, "from my dresser."

"Oh?" I said, stunned. "That?"

"I'd have given it to you," he chided gently, "if I'd known it offended you. No matter." (His mind wasn't really on me. It shouldn't have been . . . I knew that.) I asked no more questions.

Why he'd had my picture there, I'd never know. But

I was thinking that *Cora* must have stolen it, and taken it away. But why? Because she was jealous? Jealous of me and Charley Ives? How could that be? But of course she was. She had let that out. "Cousin . . . Teacher." It was possible. After all, I had thought he cared for her and was drifting back to her. Although he did not and was not, or so he contended. She could have made the mistake the other way around. We were a triangle without a base, Cora and Charley Ives and I. Jealousy. Well then, thought I excitedly, how can I use it? Small . . . human and small . . . but such a thing as jealousy, compound of love and hate, that moves the blood. How could I fit it into a role?

The girl back of the counter said, "Aren't you Olivia Hudson? Dr. Harper wants you. Room 862. Right away."

"Oh?"

"He says Miss Steffani has gone into a trance." She rolled her eyes.

We flew for the elevator.

CHAPTER 16

On the afternoon of the 20th of May (ten days after Kent Shaw's visit), Cora went through her trance performance for the sixth time. It was much like the rest. At four after 3:00 P.M., she opened her eyes and told us where she had been walking.

On a golf course, she said, that lay high on a headland projected into water. She had been wearing her dark red jacket, a gray skirt, and a gray-and-red paisley scarf around her neck. She had spoken, this time, to a golfer, an elderly man with a pure white mustache and slanted white eyebrows. "But it can't be real," she whimpered, clutching the black silk collar of her Chinese jacket. "There *is* no such thing as a *red* golf ball."

"What did you say to the man?" asked Gray with quiet intensity.

She had said her usual lines. Where am I? and so on. She threw in the usual flat statement that she had felt afraid.

"Where was this?" asked Charley Ives softly.

Why, she had been in Maine. Where in Maine? Castine.

At this word, Charley Ives and Bud Gray oozed out of the room. I think Cora was shocked to see them so

174

swiftly slip away. She was about ready to go into the weeping part, the hysteria, and she cried my name for a beginning. But her performance had become a most superficial reading. I thought she was working against a certain lassitude. But I didn't intend to stay for the aftermath.

I said shrilly, "Can't she have a sedative, Doctor? Don't let her suffer. Stop this, can't you?"

"Don't leave me, Ollie . . ." Her wail was mechanical.

"I can't stay in this room," I said to the doctor. "It scares me . . ."

I must have given a good performance because he responded helpfully, snapping, "Better go put your head down."

So I ran out of there. I ran in the corridor. I jittered in the elevator. I raced across the green carpet in the lobby. I was about to hurl myself through the revolving door when Charley and Bud came along *behind* me. I found myself flying through the door in my own compartment as if I were a badminton bird.

"You can't come," said Charley sternly in the street, but I scrambled into Bud's car with them, just the same. They had no time to argue with me. Any hope of catching Darlene Hite lay in speed, of course, so the car roared northward, to where the amphibian and its pilot waited at a small airport in Westchester. Now flying is no gypsy business, any more. But Charley and Bud had certain mysterious connections upon which I did not spy. (They had, for instance, a way to get in touch with each other through some third relay station.) Through this channel they could and did insert our sudden purpose into regulated patterns. They arranged permission to land on water, as they had foreseen might be the way to come down closest to an unknown destination.

Yet it had taken us more than an hour to become airborne and the amphibian was no jet. We would not get to Maine for hours more.

Yes, *we*. Oh, they hadn't got rid of me. It was a four-place plane. There was room. I was stubborn.

Once we were sitting still in the sky watching time turn, the flurry died and we caught our breaths. Charley said, "Cousin Ollie, why didn't you stay with her?"

"She wouldn't have said anything helpful. She just goes into a silence. You know how she does. I'll bet you one thing. This is the last stunt. She was let down, and relieved too. I think her dream-walking is all over."

"Could be," Bud agreed. "But Maine's too far. We're not going to make it, kids. This will be what is known as a wild goose chase." He stretched his legs as far as he could and sighed. His nice undistinguished face was soberly unhopeful.

"Be thankful it isn't Arizona," said Charley Ives. "And if it's our last chance all the more reason for taking it."

"Darlene's too smart," Bud said. "She's not going to hang around."

Charley had himself draped with radio connections. "If the police get her, we'll hear," he told us.

"The police in Castine?" said I. It seemed they had phoned, downstairs in the hospital. "Why, they *will*." My hope revived. "Castine's not a big place and out on

176

a point of land the way it is. . . . I've been there."

Gray was wagging his head negatively.

"If they don't," I asked, "what shall *we do?*"

"Beginning to wonder," said Charley grimly.

"Talk to this golfer, whoever he is?"

"Not a lot of use. He'll only confirm, like all the rest."

Gray roused himself somewhat. "You know, I wonder why they take the risk. Darlene, for instance, is certainly smart enough to know damn well the risk of getting caught gets greater every time and it's about maximum right now. Could be in the contract, of course, that she gets no pay until the finish of the series. Must be some such motive."

"It may be in the contract, exactly so," said Charley. "Cora took the risk, didn't she? We'll come down on water, close to the middle of town. And Ollie, I don't know what to do with you." I felt like excess baggage. "You shouldn't be seen. You're known. Picture in the papers. Darlene Hite would recognize you."

"You, too, Charley, my boy," said I.

"Not me, though," said Bud with relish. "So *I'm* the one to track down Darlene Hite." All along he'd been keenly interested in this name.

"Suppose I go see this golfer," said Charley nobly. "Pick up what I can and no harm done. But Ollie, how *you* can lie low I do not know because we'll fly in about as secretly as a zeppelin. Better tag along with me. What are you doing here, anyhow?" Charley was exasperated.

177

"I know more about Darlene Hite than either of you," said I. "She won't answer her official description, for goodness' sakes. But I know things about her she may not trouble to conceal. Her walk, her hands, way she holds her head . . ." They looked on me kindly, with only a little pity. "You may take no stock in my methods, my dear Watsons," said I, "but *I* do."

"Well," drawled Charley, "we can't throw you out."

"This hope's so damn forlorn," Bud said, meaning to be sweet to me, "let Ollie try."

"By the way, boys," said I briskly, "amateur though I am, may I ask if it's discreet to be seen chatting cozily in that snack bar? Cora's probably getting full reports on the hospital grapevine. I betcha the betting's about even among the help as to *which* side I'm spying on. How can I make her believe I am an ally when I'm hobnobbing with the enemy downstairs?"

"She's right," Bud said. He was smiling.

Charley said, "Forlorn hope. *You* can never fool Cora." He grinned and I could have slapped him. "I doubt if you could fool anybody, coz. You've got a certain transparency, and I'm not being derogatory."

"That chap, Shaw, said it pretty well," Bud put in. "A dedicated person, honest as the sun."

"Oh, pish tush!" I cried. "Little do you reck, Charley, my boy."

"Now, she's offended. There's a female for you," Bud chuckled. "Tell a lady she shines with integrity. What happens? She's just annoyed. You've maligned her femininity." He was teasing. His nice face smiled upon me fondly. Charley was silent in a thunderous kind of way.

178

"You forget," I said in a thin aloof voice. "I am not only female, but I *teach* the art of make-believe."

Charley murmured, "For the Lord's sweet sake, let's not get into that."

"Marcus," said I. We shut our mouths, both of us.

Bud Gray's thoughts went back to the job. "If I can only just cross, just once, the trail of Darlene Hite, and dig up the slightest indication to go on, I'll guarantee I'll track her." Now he seemed to be taking, if not hope, at least resolution. He and Charley began to discuss methods, how to inquire of places of lodging, depots of transportation, what ways there were to find a moving person. They were all-policemen.

I suppose we made very good time indeed. It was too slow. By six, we were still two hours away from Castine. The radio spoke to Charley. Round and about, through channels, the news was sent. Police, in Castine, knew of a man who actually used red golf balls. A certain Judge Ellsworth. They had gone to the golf course atop the hill and found him playing there. No incident. Nothing had happened there at three o'clock that afternoon. Nothing at all.

"A failure!" cried Bud Gray. "Darlene defaulted. Too smart, like I said. Bet she's a thousand miles away from Castine now." He was completely deflated, suddenly.

"Proves they are faked," I suggested feebly, "doesn't it, Charley?"

Charley was in touch with New York. He wrestled with the air waves for twenty minutes. Meanwhile, the plane droned ahead and Bud and I looked bleakly at the subtly failing light.

Charley wrenched at his gear. "It's out," he said angrily. "Through people in the hospital. Sensation," he stated bitterly.

Bud said, "What now?"

"We aren't far . . . Shall we go on?"

"Let's go on," I urged. I couldn't bear to think of turning back into the seething, the publicity. "Suppose this Judge Ellsworth is ducking, just not admitting—I wouldn't blame him. It's been ghastly for the people like Jo Crain. There may be something we can find out."

Nobody told the pilot to change the course. We flew on. We were peering ahead for the magnificence of Penobscot Bay when the radio spoke again.

"*What!*" yelped Charley. Bud and I nearly climbed into the earphones with him. Charley lit up with energy and surprise. "Here's a twist for us! The incident *happened!*"

"Happened? Did the Judge admit . . . ?"

"The Judge reported to the police at five-twenty. Woman stopped him . . . but it happened *at five o'clock!*"

"Five! Not three, but five! Two hours late!"

"Golfing! At five P.M.?"

"The old chap lives the other side of the course and *plays his way home to dinner*," said Charley.

"Slip up?" Bud Gray looked as if he would here and now *jump* the rest of the way.

But we knew, whatever it was, it gave us a chance, it cut down the margin.

"She did it," cried Bud. "Darlene Hite. *She is there.*" He yearned at the horizon.

180

Dusk was creeping in at the day's edges as we came down on the stretch of water inlet from Penobscot Bay that (and for the life of me, I'll never understand why) they call the Bagaduce River. We were certainly not inconspicuous. A boat, divorced from the shore by sheer curiosity, came out and fetched us. So we stepped up upon the dock at the base of the center of town. Charley Ives loped off, straight up the hill. Bud Gray started for the police station. I pulled my dark tweed coat close in the sharp air. I'd found a scarf in my pocket and tied it around my head. I walked away from the boatman's stare. Suddenly, all alone.

Ah, but that town is an enchanted town. Castine. Time and space conspire to give it distinction. But the long fascination of its history, the magnificence of its situation, do not entirely account for the enchantment. I knew Castine.

I turned to my left on the street at the base of the hill, thinking to myself that I had my methods. There is a store. I don't suppose any tourist ever missed it. I knew no better place to begin to look for someone who might have seen Darlene Hite. I doubted if much escaped Miss Beth, for all her professional pose of vague sweetness.

Miss Beth's Variety Store is distinguished for being a place of confusion and disorder. I've exchanged notes with people who, years after, tell about finding a box of chocolates among the overshoes, or a string of beads under a frying pan, or woolen socks in a glass lamp chimney. I bought a blue silk nightgown there, I think *because* I found it in a keg of copper paper clips. The entire store is a place where the customers root

181

happily for hours among the wares, stirring them (with no protest from Miss Beth) into even more startling juxtapositions. I don't know how Miss Beth stumbled into her peculiar way of shopkeeping, but I'm sure she is shrewd enough to know its charm and never change. Something is answered there, some vacationing rebellion against classification and discipline. Some feeling for luck, unearned. The place is always crowded with people digging and hunting and uttering cries. There, everything one buys has been discovered, like treasure.

As I well knew, Miss Beth didn't close shop at any strict hour, but drifted with the human tide. As long as people came, she kept the door open, and herself remained, aloof and faintly smiling, never nagging a body to buy or even tell her what he was looking for, seeming to assume that naturally, he would not know until he found it.

I came to the shop and went in. It was its own glorious mess. There were perhaps ten people in the place, glazed of eye, just as I remembered, pawing happily in the poor light which only enhanced the mysteries. I sought Miss Beth and said to her, "Please help me. I'm looking for a woman, about my height and weight, one who would be a stranger, but who certainly was in town today."

"I don't know, dee-ah," said Miss Beth, putting on helplessness.

"She walks," I bent from the hips forward and pulled my neck out of line with my spine, "or stands like this."

Miss Beth said, "You can't say what she'd be wearing?"

"No." She shook her head and I said, "I know it's almost impossible but I'm very anxious to find her."

"Good many women in today, dee-ah," she said with a faint air of disapproval.

"When she smokes she puts a cigarette in her mouth and smokes without fuss, without gestures." Miss Beth smiled blankly. "Her hair would be dark but she'd have it covered." It was no good. Miss Beth, if anyone, would be able to catch at these wisps of mine. I felt if she couldn't, no one could. I began to think it unlikely, anyhow, that a wily Darlene Hite would have been tempted into this store.

I looked around me helplessly. What a romantic I was. Me and my wispy unsubstantial description. What could I do? Prowl the streets? Go up the hill? Try a hotel? Professionals would be working.

"Her nose," I said with no faith, and tried describing that. But Miss Beth had lost interest and looked at me as if I didn't belong. Behind the mad tangle of a high counter, I heard a woman cry, "Look what I *found!* Henry, come look at this!" I couldn't help smiling. A word came to me. Serendipity. It's been getting a bit of use lately. I said it aloud.

Miss Beth's smile was not vacant enough to fool me. She'd know the word, for that happy quality of being able to find something you want but weren't really looking for. I then had a peculiar experience.

I suppose I was strung very tight and vibrating, and there I stood, having been transported so suddenly, so far. Stood in this store dedicated to serendipity. And I was besides, in that enchanted town, that for mystical and inexplicable reasons had always seemed to me to be a place to *find* things. What I felt was a surge of absolutely unwarranted hope. Surely if there was magic, it would work for me. I thought, very well. One had only to fall into the rhythm, the joyful expectancy of the unexpected, a mood in which one does not push anxiously or narrowly. One opens and becomes ready for luck. One lets it happen.

I don't know yet. I still think it was the nearest thing to supernatural I've ever known. I smiled at Miss Beth and said to her placidly, "I'm not quite sure what I want. May I just look around?"

It was an unnecessary question. Her business was built on it.

So I turned and felt hope stir. Anything . . . anything might be hidden here, mixed in somewhere. As, indeed, anything may be hidden in the great world itself, confused and roaring as it is, upon which men spin and invent their feeble lanes of plan and purpose. But the great globe is a buzz, a throbbing, swiftly shimmering fabric of intermeshed acts, and it cannot be all charted. How do you know what you want until you find it? thought I, in that strange reverie, and turned my head and saw Kent Shaw walk by in the street.

CHAPTER 17

Serendipity? I was struck stock still. *Kent Shaw!* Why *here?* He couldn't have heard about Cora's latest dream and beaten us here. He couldn't have come, *having heard.* So did he know in advance? Or was he visiting relatives? Coincidence? No, no. I'd found something!

I slipped quietly out of Miss Beth's and looked to my left. Kent's topcoated figure was moving rapidly along the street. I followed him. You don't quarrel, you don't question. I'd got into the mood to be led, and so I followed.

The street becomes what you could call a road. The road follows the water. The hill went up to my right, across the way. On the water side there is a little museum, old Fort Pentagoet. I followed Kent Shaw along that road until, before the museum itself, closed of course at this hour, he stopped walking. He was obviously disposing himself to wait.

Deep dusk had by now fallen on this side of the hill. I slipped behind a huge shrub, twenty yards away, and stood still, tingling. Was it a rendezvous?

Kent Shaw, here! In Castine, Maine? For the first time, there came into my mind the question I'd never

185

asked myself, although I had heard Marcus make the remark that demanded it. "Someone very clever has designed this thing," the old wizard had said. The question should have followed. *Who, then?* Who had invented this plot? Who devised it? Who masterminded it? Not Cora Steffani. I'd been right when I said she wasn't that clever. Darlene Hite was an unknown quantity, of course, but obscure. And Raymond Pankerman and his money were not in her ken. Nor could he have designed the plot, pudgy-brained Raymond. Where had he acquired the experience or the imagination or the skill to devise such a scheme and direct it and make it work? But Kent Shaw! He *was* capable. In fact, the whole thing was just like him!

I had found something. I had found the brains. I was convinced without any proof. I shifted from foot to foot behind that shrub, wild with excitement.

And Kent Shaw waited by the museum door. I could just see him. I could sense that he, too, danced with anxiety. I could see his arm whip out and strike at the small hedging plants beside the museum entrance. Those movements in the near dark expressed a furious impatience.

I didn't know what to do. A few cars drifted by, their headlights froze him momentarily to something still and anonymous. But there were no pedestrians. Yet he was waiting for something. Some*one,* of course. I felt sure it was Darlene, who, in a plan, was going to meet him there. And I, Olivia Hudson, 34, teacher, female, amateur, was watching, all alone.

This, however, wasn't so for long. Something said

my name so softly I thought it was a dream. Said it again a trifle more robustly. I became aware of Bud Gray standing close behind me, sheltered, also, in the lee of that bush. He had called my attention skillfully, without alarming me. In a moment, I was clutching his coat and whispering joyfully into his bending ear.

"Shaw? That him? Okay. We'll see."

I had much excited putting of clues together that I could not possibly whisper, then. But oh, I was glad that he had come.

We waited. The night air was chilly, but it had, as air has in that place, its own peculiar invigorating clarifying quality. Every breath seems to soothe and rearrange the very cells of the brain. I *knew* I had found something.

Meanwhile, the figure of Kent Shaw moved restlessly in a tiny orbit. He kept hitting out at those shrubs, as if pressure inside needed the relief of the gesture. We stood there what seemed hours. Hours. No car stopped. Nobody walked by.

"She isn't coming," I whispered, cramped, stiff, and beginning to despair.

"Doesn't seem so." Too smart, Bud was thinking and I knew his thought.

We could tell Kent Shaw was on the point of giving up and I was wild. "She isn't coming," I repeated. "Oh, pity . . . pity. But we can't miss a chance like this, Bud. Listen, why don't *I* go? I think I can fool him for a moment, anyhow. If he thinks I'm Darlene Hite, maybe he'll speak. It could give us something."

"Careful," said Bud Gray, holding me.

"It's all right. You can watch, or come behind.

Then you can hear if he does speak. Bud, let me try to fool him, for even a second or two. Otherwise, he's going to leave and we won't know anything."

"Try it," Bud said abruptly and shoved me a little.

So I tried to put myself in Darlene's skin. I didn't know the role very well. I had such wispy clues, such slight indications. All I had, I tried to use—to walk carrying my head as I'd been told she did—to think of myself as cool and business-like. I had ready in my throat the syllable of his name. I hadn't taken ten steps around that shrub when Kent Shaw saw my figure moving toward him in the dimness and his restlessness jelled to motionless attention.

I thought, It's going to work!

Then I saw the woman crossing the road. I don't know where she came from. I wished I could wait until she was by. She was a hulk in a coat that bloomed at the hips like an old-fashioned dolman and she walked splay-footed. I hadn't far to go. I tried to slow my steps and stall my approach until this lonely figure should pass me by, for she crossed on a diagonal and would come walking toward me, between me and Kent Shaw. She wore a decrepit felt hat pulled down on her brows.

We would pass. Then I would hear what Kent Shaw might say to Darlene Hite. I thought, surely Darlene would stall as I am stalling, so it will work. It will be all right.

But just as she came abreast of me, and we were not thirty feet from Kent's silent shape, that woman whipped out a flashlight and threw its beam full into my face. She said in a Down East twang, "'Tain't smart

188

to walk here alone by night, dee-ah. Don't you know no better?"

"Don't do that," I murmured, blinking, exposed. I grabbed for her wrist and turned the beam. It fell on her face. Her eyes were shrewd little slits. Her hair was white, her brows disorderly and pale. So much I saw, when she let go the button and the light went out.

"Should know better," she said severely. "Git back where there's folks."

I could have scratched and bitten her! I muttered something and swiveled around her. The light had ruined my vision. But I knew, bitterly I knew, Kent Shaw had gone.

Then Bud Gray was pinching my arm. He took out a flash of his own and lit it. "Oh damn!" I was almost crying. *Damn* that old busybody! Do you see him, Bud? Where did he go?"

Bud said, professionally undismayed, "No telling, Ollie. Too bad." He turned his light on the museum door.

"He can't be in there!" I cried. "I thought I saw his shadow. Didn't you? Maybe he ducked up the hill. Can't we follow?"

Bud tried the door. It was locked. He turned the beam of light. "What would we say if we caught up with him? He can be found, Ollie. That's no problem."

"Damn, damn, damn old biddy!" I raged.

"Maybe you were lucky," Bud said.

"What?"

"Look there."

I saw the small hedge, then, in the light. Saw how the low shrubs had been cut and mutilated. I remembered the slashing of Kent Shaw's hand. I said, "What do you mean?"

"He had a knife, I'm guessing, aren't you?" Bud said. "And a darned sharp one, at that."

The night was very cold. I hadn't noticed the cold so much before. Bud put his arm around me and I was grateful for the warmth and the shelter of it. We began to walk back toward the shops. It looked a long dark chilly way. No one was abroad. The dwelling houses were smug and tight, with blinds drawn. The old biddy who had swung that light into my face was not to be seen ahead of us. No doubt she was safe from the hazards of the night behind the blinds in one of the houses. Neither was Kent Shaw to be seen behind us, or anywhere.

Bud said, "I must get on the phone. You'd better be someplace warm."

"Kent saw my face," I said through chattering teeth, "and ran away. Do you think he knows I knew *he* was there?"

"No telling."

"Where did he go? What will he do?"

"No telling that, either. Can we go a little faster?"

"Go ahead," I said. "You need to hurry. I'm holding you back."

"Don't like to leave you," he objected.

"You'll start a hunt for him? Try to catch him?" I stumbled along as fast as I could beside him.

"No use to catch him. But I want him watched."

"Darlene didn't come," I panted. "Why didn't she?"

"Because she's smart."

"He had a knife for *her?* That's what you think? And she'd guessed he would?"

Bud said, "If he *is* the brains and made the plot then he is the killer. I didn't think Darlene Hite killed Ed Jones. I dunno, I never could believe that. Kent Shaw suits me a lot better."

"But he would have *killed* her? *There?* In front of that museum? A corpse with Cora's nose—wouldn't that . . . ? I can't understand what he meant to do."

"The water is near enough," Bud said. "And a knife is not only quiet, but handy for remodeling."

I was so shocked and revolted, I nearly fell and he had to hold me up with both arms. Footsteps rang on cement. We could see the shape of Charley Ives coming in his characteristic lope out of light and shadow ahead. "You all right?" Bud said. "Sorry. I said that pretty brutally."

"I'm all right. And here's Charley. You hurry." I thrust his arms away and tried to stand by myself.

"Anything wrong?" asked Charley.

"Take her other arm," said Bud. "Get back to the police station. Hurry."

So they almost carried me. My feet did not seem to touch the ground. While I was being whisked along, Bud told my cousin Charley, in quick short sentences, what had happened.

"Whah . . . !" said Charley. I seemed to rise a foot above the earth on the impulse of his excitement. "Kent Shaw! This is our break! Good girl, Ollie. How did you get on to him?"

"Serendipity," I giggled, impelled toward hysterical mirth by my ridiculous rate of progress and the aftershock of danger.

"The whole damn scheme has practically got his signature on it," Charley cried. "His style, eh?"

I remember saying, tearfully (hysterically), "Why Charley, my boy, that's pretty arty talk for you."

He paid no attention.

"You can see why he's got to get rid of Darlene," Bud said. "Now that it's over, he's scared she'll talk. And if she does, he's in for it, for Ed Jones. Darlene must know that."

"She knows all right," Charley proclaimed joyfully. "Listen to this. Judge Ellsworth meets this dame on the golf course. She wants to know where she is and he tells her. Then she says, 'My name is Cora Steffani and somebody wants to kill me.' Then she runs away."

"What!" Bud's excitement made him stop still and I was stretched between them like a rag on a washline. "Why?" yelped Bud.

"Why *say* that?" Now Charley stopped and Bud moved and I fluttered in the middle. "Because Kent Shaw has also got to get rid of Cora. Darlene is warning her. He's a killer and those two women both know it."

They, then, plucked me up, with no more pretense that I was in any way walking, and ran up the steps to the police station.

CHAPTER 18

We didn't leave Castine until late the following morning. Darlene Hite had not been found.

Judge Ellsworth, who was seventy-three, retired, and the real thing in a golf fanatic, used red balls because he often played so early in the northern spring that sometimes there was still snow on the ground. He played whenever he felt like it, which was nearly always. But the one inflexible thing about it was his habit of playing four holes, always alone, on his way home to his six o'clock dinner.

He was a bit confused when we talked to him that evening, refusing to identify *me* as the woman he had seen. When we straightened that out, he still refused to identify Cora's pictures. He said it was nonsense and a great nuisance and he didn't want to hear any more about it.

He did tell us that when the woman spoke to him he recognized the scene (since the police had already asked him whether it *had* happened). So he was, he said, suspicious. But all alone. And very much annoyed at becoming one of Cora's victims. He had not pursued her when she ran away. He had marched on home to his phone and simply called the police.

Cora walks again, the papers shrieked. *Dream Walker in Maine.* The time discrepancy was fuel, that's all, for heated argument. The red golf balls were "color." But the sentence the woman in Maine had said, that the woman in New York had *not* reported (Somebody wants to kill me.), that was *sensation!* The story rolled . . . nothing could stop its momentum now.

But we, of course, pondered these details.

Kent Shaw. Who, we said to each other, had turned up in the very beginning and seen to it that the very first incident in the series had been carefully recorded before witnesses for future reference?

Who had somewhat unnaturally withdrawn, and taken care not to be seen with Cora any more?

Who had written her a cryptic note from Los Angeles, which I tried frantically to quote? Who had *been* in Los Angeles at the time of Ed Jones' murder? Who had the chance to signal, on TV?

Who had told Cora that she could go abroad in ten days time, ten days ago?

Who could have known both women? Who had the fantastical imagination, the genius, the half-mad brain for the job? Kent Shaw. Kent Shaw. He answered *all* of this.

And who, finally, had turned up in Castine—with a knife? Oh, we were convinced, and afraid to be convinced. We had no proof of any kind whatsoever.

The three of us, exhausted, were sitting in the air being carried back. "Why did he want to meet Darlene in Maine?" I asked.

"Thought it was safer. Couldn't guess *we'd* get there that fast. Safer than a meeting in New York would be." Charley was ready with suggestions.

"Why did he make it so long after the golf course bit?"

"Wasn't so long after five o'clock."

"Then you think the bit on the golf course was *supposed* to happen at five?"

"I sure do," said Bud. "Because that's the old chap's one invariable habit. And that's when he'd have no spry young companion."

"How did Cora make a mistake?" I wondered. "If it were *written down*," said I, "a five and a three are not always unlike. They must have had it written down. How could they remember the tiny things, exact words, clothes, everything? Did you ever search . . . ?" They looked upon me with kindness. "Nothing?" I queried. "Did you look *everywhere*? In the hospital, too?" They looked upon me with patience.

"Got to blow the lid off the entire thing," said Charley, "to explain the one detail that matters."

"The blue envelope," said I.

"Exactly. That's the one."

"Kent Shaw put it in the book. Heavens, Charley, he's always mooching around trying to sell his stuff."

"If we can prove that . . ." This was our hope. Charley would try.

"What will Kent do now?" I worried.

"We'll watch and see."

"Can't let him really kill anybody."

"That's right. Neither woman. For Marcus' sake, if no other. Guards already on the hospital. Don't worry."

"You think," said I, "he arranged this rendezvous a long time ago. Did he know *then* he'd want to kill her? And set the time after dark?"

"He'd want it dark enough not to be seen," Bud said, "in any case."

"But why a rendezvous at all?"

"For the pay-off?" Charley said.

"Now she knows it's dangerous, but how is she going to ever get paid off?"

"Aaaah," said Bud Gray.

"She must *expect* to get paid," I insisted, "or she wouldn't have risked that golf course bit and finished the job."

"Aaaah," said Bud again and drew his head into his collar like a turtle and fell to thinking.

Charley said, "Much as I'd like to lay about me with Kent Shaw's name, I think we'll first have to see what we can get by watching him. We are supposing, aren't we, that he would like to kill two women? One of them is where we can watch her. And he may yet lead us to the other one." Bud sighed.

"No need to be downhearted," said Charley, "our position shows a lot of improvement."

"If it hadn't been for that chaperone type," I fretted. "If I could have gotten one word out of him, if he had called me by Darlene's name, even . . . that would really have been an improvement."

"If he'd stuck his knife in you," said Charley, "better yet?" Then he exuded a kind of deep and dangerous silence.

"Why, Bud was there," said I. (But oh, Kent Shaw could have killed me and I quivered to think of it, coward that I am.)

Charley stretched like a big cat. "Might have expected something of the sort. Had you thought of it, Bud? Did you let her take the risk, blind?"

"She'd have taken the risk," Bud said firmly.

"I don't doubt she would," said my cousin Charley. "She'd get carried away by the part."

"*I* doubt it," snapped I.

Bud said, ignoring me, "You make choices in this business."

"I agree," said Charley Ives stiffly, "but I can't admire taking advantage of Ollie's dramatic instincts."

I was annoyed. "I don't *believe* Bud knew he had a knife. I'm *sure* I didn't."

"You better stick to your trade," he said. "Stay around the hospital. Cora's going to be under pressure and possibly . . ."

"Indulge my dramatic instincts there, you mean?"

"Uh huh."

"Make-believe?" said I, getting madder.

"That's right," said Charley Ives.

"I think you're jealous," I cried. I was thinking that I, the amateur, had had all the luck, and seen Kent Shaw.

Charley said, "That I deny. Jealousy is a rotten—" He shut up suddenly.

"It sure is," I murmured, thinking of Cora. "If Cora

was a 'woman scorned,' " I blurted. "Oh, Charley, you shouldn't have kept on hanging around her."

"Teach me," said Charley, in muted anguish.

I bit my tongue and tasted blood.

"You are right," said Charley evenly, "and I was wrong."

Gray said something about some department and they began to use quick names and expressions I didn't know. They were being professional over my head.

I shrank in my seat, feeling miserable. Me, the blundering amateur, who had the luck—but not the sense to keep my mouth shut. Of course, Charley blamed himself, and why did I have to be the detestable type who pointed things out and was "right"? I pretended to sleep.

When we got back to town, my escorts left me flat to go set up the machinery. They were calmer than I. They knew that patience and effort would turn up something useful. They were trained to take a hypothesis, like the involvement of Kent Shaw, and go to work to test it.

I knew some of the plans. People would try to find a connection between Kent Shaw and Raymond Pankerman. (They never did.)

Try to find out if and when Kent Shaw had got into Charley's place while the book in which the blue envelope was found was lying there waiting to be shipped to Marcus. (They found nothing like evidence; only the possibility.)

Inquire in Los Angeles about Kent Shaw on the night of the murder of Jones. (Nothing.)

Investigate his finances, check on his long distance calls, his travels. (Too long, too late.)

Go back in his career to see where his path had crossed Darlene Hite's. (And this they found, but what was it but another possibility?)

Of course, possibilities pile up, but it was going to be a long slow swell, and meanwhile Marcus could only deny any knowledge of the blue envelope. But he couldn't *explain,* and the story roared, frothed, spit. . . .

I went home. I let myself into my own place and looked at my books and my records, my paintings, my bric-a-brac, my ivory tower. I prayed that in some way, I, from my isolation, in my feebleness, had yet a use. But all my ideas were, I sadly recognized, strictly theatrical.

This was the 21st of May. I called the hospital. Cora would take no calls, see no one. I spoke to Dr. Harper. He told me that they were in a state of siege and that the board insisted that Cora had to be kicked out of there. "Disrupts our work, hurts our reputation, name suffers, people are upset. Can't go on. Charley Ives sold me a bill of goods in the first place. Had no idea what we were in for." He was fuming.

"You can't just throw her out into the street," said I, alarmed, thinking of Kent Shaw.

"She claims it's all over because wild horses couldn't drag another word from her lips. If she ever has another dream nobody will know it. Oh, she's a fraud, Miss Olivia."

"Where can she go?" I was worried.

"She's got an apartment. Oh, she's in a panic. Doesn't want to go there. We've got guards here, as a matter of fact. And it's intolerable."

"She has to be safe, for Marcus' sake."

"I suppose so," the doctor admitted gloomily. "She speaks of going abroad as soon as she can get the money."

"The money?" I pricked up my ears.

"I've half a mind to give her the money to get rid of her."

"Oh, no. Don't you do that. Remind her of *me*."

"If you want to get in to see her," he growled, "I'll see that you do."

"No. I'd rather *she* let me in," said I.

Staunch old friend. It was a phony characterization.

When I called Marcus, he was cheerful. He knew all that Charley knew. So I told him about my strange experience in Miss Beth's store. "It was odd, Uncle John. What I'd like to know . . . did I feel prophetically hopeful because I was going to see Kent Shaw? Or did I see Kent Shaw because I felt hopeful?"

"Good girl, Ollie. You saw him because you felt hopeful, I should say."

"But wasn't it a coincidence?"

"Coincidence means only a connection that's not seen. Roots meet underground. And hope is creative. Look at it this way. Suppose you'd stood there without hope, bewailing a stone wall. You'd have been blind. He could have walked by without your noticing."

"Hope is creative?" said I. "How can that be?"

"I don't know how," said Marcus. "I only perceive that it is."

200

So he passed me some courage. While the papers bled ink, the talk careened dangerously, giddily on, and Marcus was being soiled and stained and disrespectful words cannot entirely be eaten, ever. Respect is a kind of Humpty Dumpty. All the King's horses can't put it all the way up, again.

Please, if I am making this clear at all, please do read the fine print and the follow-up and all the hard, dry parts in the news. Don't let your mind jump on to the next sensational headline. Oh, it's more fun to float along, enjoying the high spots. The new murder. The latest scandal. Today's clash. But afterwards, people have to live. And if all you remember is a vague impression of some nasty mess, and the thing that remains is only your notion that this person once fell away from the clear and unquestioned way—and to know what truly did happen is a task too dry, too hard —ah, please. It isn't fair.

Secretary, whoever you are. Delete the paragraph above. I mustn't bleat. I don't think I'm feeling very well. . . . Tomorrow, if I have tomorrow . . . I can finish this. Start a new chapter. . . .

CHAPTER 19

I don't mean to drag you through all the anguish we suffered, being ignorant. So I will try to follow my original intention and go backstage, and tell how the four who were in the plot were moving in what to us was darkness.

I will go back to Darlene Hite. Once she realized (after the discovery of the body of Ed Jones, on March 28th) that Kent Shaw was a killer, Darlene saw ahead. She saw what was written on the wall because she was smart. And because she had been in the jungle. Kent Shaw, who had killed a man just to save his beautiful scheme intact, would not hesitate to eliminate her, either, once her job was finished. So Darlene considered her position.

She was not required to do anything in Washington, on the 5th of May. (This incident, she knew nothing about.) Her script called only for an appearance in Castine on May 20th. That would be the end of it. She was to meet her boss afterwards and collect her handsome reward and live happily ever after.

But Darlene, having read the papers and well-considered the future, wished to take care of Darlene. So she left New Orleans, early in April, went to Toronto, and there, early in May, she found a surgeon and had her nose remodeled.

Now the doctor in Toronto read the papers, too. When, after I'd gone to Los Angeles, after the 5th of May, we broke forth the suspicion that a certain Darlene Hite might be involved in Cora's huge hoax, and when we published her pictures, you would think he'd speculate about this patient. Maybe he did. But the pictures were old, and, as I say, retouched for glamour, and furthermore, *he believed the third witness in the park in Washington*. The doctor thought Darlene Hite had been seen in Washington on the 5th of May. So how could she be his patient, whom he was even then attending? He didn't even mention it. She had another name, a cover story, and plenty of "expense" money. He did not wish to embarrass her.

So Darlene lay low and healed. She read what was supposed to have happened to Marcus and knew it hadn't. She may have dimly recognized the crux of the plot. But Darlene, as I think I've said before, had a narrow view and the meaning of John Paul Marcus was neither apparent nor important to her. She was looking after Darlene, and doing it very well, too.

In good time, she "vanished" from Toronto. She evolved a new character. Bleached her hair back to its original blond or even whiter. Bleached her brows. Took off assorted supporting garments. Practiced a new waddling walk. Bought elderly oxfords, those dreadful shoes that are offered to women over fifty as a matter of course.

She went to New York, and foxily smoothed out a future way there. She took off for Castine two weeks early. On May 20th, at 5:00 P.M. (the figure Cora took for a three in the script, after all this time), Darlene used a black fringe of artificial hair under the scarf and very easily vanished to a prepared identity, after that stunt was over.

But she had ad-libbed. She had warned Cora Steffani, as best she could, for she knew that Cora's elimination was also written on the wall.

Now, Darlene's problem was to collect her wages and live to enjoy them.

She had kept the rendezvous with Kent Shaw before the museum. But we interfered. She'd seen us. She was hoping Bud and I would go away. She was watching, when I stepped out from behind that shrub. She could tell as well as I that Kent Shaw had been fooled, for a moment. *She* knew he was dangerous. She may even have known he held that knife for she could expect a knife. So Darlene acted. Stepped out from some ambush of her own, crossed the road, and threw that beam of light in my face, to save my life.

Darlene Hite, of course, was the old biddy in the dolman. But her nose, as we had been able to see so plainly when I turned the light on her, was no longer anything like Cora's nose. I did not recognize her. (Me and my methods! Me and my vanities!)

But she didn't get the key. Key to some deposit box where her money lay hidden and waiting for her. The key Kent Shaw was promising to deliver that night in front of the little museum, in the dark and the cold.

Darlene had guessed easily enough what he'd rather deliver. She had a gun under that dolman. She'd hoped to surprise him, to take the key away, and vanish, as she was so skilled in doing. Then conquer the problem of safely reaching that box—thereafter to disappear forever.

But she had found herself saving my life, instead.

Darlene was no killer, nor did she want to see anyone killed. When she saw me on that dim sidewalk, living, and so close to dying, it was no abstraction, either. Darlene was shaken. For the first time, she glimpsed the fact that taking care of Darlene might mean taking care of other people, also. And not letting murder go. But she skipped out of Castine in her own invisible way. There was her pay.

She came to New York where she had deep-laid some alternate plans. At that time, she was wondering how to expose all but herself, thinking in terms of anonymous letters. She didn't want to appear. She wanted her well-earned money. She'd better get that first, she thought. She would try for it, once more.

None of this did we know.

Now Raymond Pankerman, watching the big impossible lie stir up the country to a frenzy, must have been laughing. I suppose it was the bright spot in his days. Yet I wonder whether he had the imagination or the sensitivity to know what had been done to Marcus. I wonder if he was satisfied. At any rate, he paid off. The combination to Kent Shaw's safe was to be forwarded, lacking a countermand, by relays through innocent people. Kent Shaw knew where it lay ready for him. But he was either too smart or too preoccupied to go near it. If he had, he might have been pounced upon. For he was watched.

He had been picked up at Boston airport, on his

way down. He'd come back to his rooming house. He did not seem to move.

I can imagine how he was preoccupied. Now, he saw himself and his beautiful hoax at the mercy of his fellow conspirators. He could understand the pressure upon them, especially the women. He wanted them silent forever. But he could not murder a woman he couldn't even locate. For Darlene, he could only wait, holding the only lure he had, her money. The other woman, however, was very conspicuously located. He knew where Cora was.

So Kent Shaw, in the shabby room among the clutter of his souvenirs, kept to his surface poverty and brooded, schemed, thought. How was he going to murder Cora in the well-protected hospital room? Especially since the whole world had been told somebody was going to try?

He was very clever, that mad little man.

Now, about Cora. She was terrified. She was in a terrible spot. She knew Kent wanted to kill her. She could no longer duck or dodge the fact that he *had* killed Ed Jones. If, to save her own life, she broke down and revealed the plot, she herself was an accessory to that killing. How could she meet Kent Shaw and collect *her* money, fearing him as she did? Even if she had *her* key, how could she go for the money, since her face was as well known to the public as any face alive? The thing had gotten out of hand. The hospital threatened to throw her out. She was afraid. She wanted to run to another continent, and hide. What could she use for money?

I'd divined that money was the crux of her problem. Pressure was on her to call for me.

Nevertheless, on the 21st, nothing moved. Everything seemed to have come to a stop.

On the 22nd there were some ripples. Mildred Garrick came to see me. Oh, I'd been seen by the Press. The white light that beat on all concerned did not skip me. I played my poor part, said foolish things. I had to. I sent most of them away puzzled or sad. But Mildred had something to tell me.

"Cora's been writing letters. Did you know? Did you advise her?"

"I haven't seen her since—"

"She wrote this note to Jo Crain."

I read the copy she handed me. I blazed. It was as if Cora thought she could get out gracefully by the exercise of just a little charming politeness. She was like a child putting on manners. "Look how good I am being now!" Sweet words, brave apologies, daintily done. I was furious. She didn't, as Charley had said, have a political thought in her head, or a moral one, either. She didn't know the meaning of "accessory before or after the fact" or of "shalt not bear false witness" or any other rule connected with her fellow men. All she knew was that Marcus was famous. She didn't know why. She herself wanted to be famous, period. She hadn't cared why. Greedy for attention, money, and a bit of revenge, she knew not what she did. She couldn't even conceive that the affair of the blue envelope would live after her. She said in that note, oh sweetly, that she intended to go away and surely it would all be forgotten. She didn't even consider that her country-men would need to know *and must know* what the truth was about Marcus.

Oh, I raged. I walked up and down my carpet and let fly with a good deal of this. Mildred patted the thing in her hair, today, that looked like a huge amber teething ring to me. "Well, well," said she. "All as I can say is, you look like you're changing sides and getting over to the unpopular one again."

"What do you mean?" I yelled at her.

"It's edging around," said Mildred. Her eyes looked tired suddenly and I could see the fine lines under her hearty make-up. "I printed this letter in my column this morning."

"You didn't!"

"Did," Mildred shrugged. "It's a job, honey."

"Jo Crain gave you that? What is Jo thinking of?"

"Nobody's going to know what Jo is thinking without Jo wants them to know," said Mildred vulgarly. "I wanted to know what you'd think and I guess I got it. Kinda hope it will make a few more folks mad."

"Don't quote *me*, please." I was alarmed.

"Boring from within, huh?" said Mildred cheerfully. "Listen, Ollie, I hold no brief for Cora—that little twerp of a half-baked Duse, believe me. But I got a job and I got an ear and I'm telling you, sympathy is edging around."

"How can it?"

"It stuck to Marcus longer than you'd expect. People don't want idols kicked over. But their sympathy is a jumpy thing. You know what's doing it? The hospital threatening to throw her out."

"Oh me," I mourned. "Mildred, leave me out of your column and out of your vocabulary for a little while? I'll . . . maybe I can give you a scoop," I offered feebly.

Mildred grinned. "You're quaint. Well, something has got to give pretty soon," she announced with great good sense. "Cheer up, Hudson. I've been known to keep my mouth shut. Boy, is this a mess!" she added with glee.

I tried to call Charley after she had left. I couldn't reach him. (He and Bud Gray never had given me, the amateur, that mysterious phone number of theirs, through which they could be reached, it seemed, about any time.)

Only a ripple. But Mildred had printed Cora's letter to Jo Crain. And Kent Shaw had read it in the paper. We didn't . . . couldn't . . . see the ripple as it enlarged.

Charley called me that evening, of the 22nd. Kent Shaw had come to the hospital late in the day. He had been watched, avidly. But he had paced the lobby a little while, looking nervous and undecided. He had gone away without even trying to get upstairs to the 8th floor.

Actually, he was checking on a point of hospital routine. This foray was a consequence of Mildred's column. We didn't know.

But I will tell you. He watched the florist's boy. Saw how an offering for Cora Steffani was stopped at the desk and looked into. Saw that the boy then put it on the elevator. And knew what to do.

On the 23rd, Darlene moved. She placed a classified ad for the Monday morning paper.

On the 24th, Kent Shaw moved. He knew as well as I did that Jo Crain was both thoughtful of her friends and an extremely important and busy person. He knew that her florist had her cards and was used to her ways. So, since Kent Shaw wasn't a bad mimic, himself, on Monday the 24th, he used Jo's secretary's voice to order red gladioli, in a basket, to be sent at exactly 4:00 P.M. to Cora Steffani in the hospital.

On the 24th, then, Kent Shaw came into the hospital lobby a little earlier than 4:00. Again he jittered, paced, and then he seemed to decide. He stepped into an elevator. Got off at the 8th floor. Bit his fingers, looked left and right, swung on his heel and rode down again, without having tried to get into Cora's room.

The guards who had watched prayerfully (Let him try!) thought he was scared off, perhaps having spotted them or sensed tension. Did not imagine what had happened between floors, in the elevator. And the glass jar of candy that Kent Shaw had carefully saturated with the same poison that had killed Ed Jones, rode into Cora's room in the midst of the blood-red gladioli in their open basket, under Jo Crain's card.

But the ripples from his act went a little differently from his expectation. Cora was put in utter terror by the news of those two visits, the second one closer than the first. (Which news she received, of course, on the hospital grapevine.) And Cora was in no mood for candy. She wasn't poisoned yet, at 6:00 P.M. on the 24th, when she called me on the phone.

CHAPTER 20

I'd been feeling like a cat on a leash, alone all the week-end and alone the Monday, that 24th of May. When I hung up on Cora, called Charley Ives and got him, I was about to pop with the release of something having happened.

"I'm convinced she's going to ask me for a loan," said I excitedly, "so what shall I do, Charley? Shall I promise to lend her the money?"

"To run away with? She can't be let go, coz."

"I know," I said, "but there's such a thing as the torture of hope. If she thinks she's escaping and then can't . . ."

Charley sounded amused. "Spanish Inquisition has nothing on you."

"Charley, my boy," I bristled.

"I don't think it matters," he cut in.

"It matters this much. If I refuse she'll, sure as fate, throw me out right away and then what use would I be?"

"Tell her anything you want," said Charley indulgently. "Except one thing. Don't twit her with Kent Shaw's name. He was up on the 8th floor yesterday. Didn't see her. But if we get Darlene tonight, we may be able to bring them all three together and I'd just as soon—"

"Get Darlene! What do you mean?"

There was a silence that shouted surprise. "Didn't Bud call you?" asked my cousin Charley rather cautiously.

"Nobody has called me for days and days," I cried indignantly. "I might as well be unconscious."

So Charley told me about the ad in the morning paper. It was addressed to K.S. and it was signed by D. Charley didn't doubt who had placed it. Neither did I. It asked K.S. to bring "key" to Biltmore lobby, 9-10 P.M. It added, "Uncle anxious to hear."

I suppose I squealed like a teen-ager.

"K.S. is going to have to go," Charley said with satisfaction.

"Are you going?"

"Not me and not you, coz," Charley said, reading my mind. "Kent knows us too well. Bud's going."

"He's met Bud."

"Once. Bud won't be very noticeable. I figure on getting into Shaw's room while he's safely out of it. What occurs to me . . . the very last thing he'll take to any rendezvous with Darlene is that so-called 'key.' Once she got that, she'd really vanish. He'd never have an easy moment thereafter. She wants him in a public place and she may threaten. You see the threat in that ad, don't you?"

"Uncle Sam?" said I.

"Exactly. So he'll give in, agree, but say the key has to be fetched and he'll want her to go some other place where it's lonelier."

"She won't *go?*"

"It won't matter. Bud will move in as soon as they meet. Point I'm making . . . who knows what I might not find in his room?"

"Can I come there?"

"Nope. You're going to the hospital and play games with Cora."

"Charley, if you get Darlene you'll come *there?*"

"Sure will."

"All right," I said. "I'll stay in the audience. I hope there's a show."

Charley said, taking pity, I suppose, because I sounded so forlorn, "Have you talked to Marcus today? Do you know he says Darlene has had her nose bobbed?"

"He does? But Charley, how could she? When would she have time? And with everyone looking for her, wouldn't that be suspicious? I don't see . . ."

"Marcus just says Judge Ellsworth isn't an old fuss-budget defending his privacy, but an honest and accurate man. And if the Judge says the woman on the golf course didn't look like Cora, then she didn't."

"But . . . does that help us any?"

"They are rounding up reports on every nose-remodeling job done over the country in the last couple of months. Can't be too many. May help." (Eventually, of course, it did.)

I said, "Thanks for all the news, Charley, my—" I stopped myself in the middle.

But Charley said, and he sounded a bit miffed, "Oh, I'm your boy, Teacher. *I* don't see why you shouldn't have the news."

He saw, I guess, later.

When I went down the corridor toward Cora's room it was 8:00 P.M. I'd made it as late as I conscionably could, so as to be around if there were going to be fireworks. I was trying to put myself into the staunch old friend pose but when I opened the door she threw me a cue for a better role.

Cora was dressed neatly in gray jersey, had her glasses on, looked very business-like. She said, "Ollie, how are you? Will you have one?"

She had a small glass jar in her hand and she was twisting the top open. "One what?" I said and she turned it and let me read the label. *Old-Fashioned Humbugs,* the label said. I looked up, at her face.

"Or shall we be honest, for a change?" she said.

"By all means," said I. I thought for a moment she was going to confess to me, then and there.

But she said, "I appreciate your 'standing by,' Ollie, darling, even if I do know you belong to the unbelievers. You think I'm a humbug, don't you?"

"And you think *I'm* a humbug," said I slowly. "Well, that should clear the air."

She put the candy down. It had been a prop for her little scene, but now the bit was over, we both forgot the candy. She in her purpose. I in the glimmer I then had of a role I might play that would drive her wild. I wanted to turn it over in my mind, taste it and test it. At the same time, I found myself laying a foundation for it.

I sat down quietly. "What do you want?"

"I want some money." (I said nothing.) "And you have plenty of money," she said a trifle waspishly.

214

"You want me to finance your departure from these shores?"

"You must see that if I leave the country all this will be a nine days' wonder and then die down. Isn't that a good thing?"

I held on to my temper. "It won't help Marcus much," I said, very flatly.

"Charley Ives seems to blame *me*. But he most certainly can't blame *you*, Ollie. Now can he?"

She seemed to have Charley Ives on a salver and be handing him over. I thought she looked gray in the face.

"You're scared, aren't you?" I leaned back.

"Of course, I'm scared. I want to get away. They won't keep me here and I'd go out of my mind if they did. I *can't* go stay in my apartment. I'd be . . . I'd be at the mercy of the curious. . . ."

"They have no mercy," I muttered, thinking we both meant Kent Shaw.

"Ollie, will you help me? I know no reason why you should. But I ask you to and I need to know."

I didn't meet her eye. (I felt, in spite of everything, like a dirty traitor.) "Oh, I already have," I said, carelessly. "I can get you a seat on a transatlantic plane tomorrow morning. You can be in Paris with modest funds—I don't say I'm going to support you forever—by the day after."

Then she sat down. I saw tension draining out of her. She thanked me in that business-like way, and she told me I would be repaid. But I could tell that she was wondering *why*.

So I talked idly. "You realize you may be hounded,

215

even there? Your destination will be no secret. How are you going to get to the plane? Do you mind an escort of newshawks? Because you are sure to have it."

"I don't mind," she said and indeed she didn't. The thought cheered her up. It should be safe. "Once I get to France," she said confidently, "I can manage to disappear."

"Like Darlene Hite," I murmured.

She said, "Ollie, whatever you believe, believe this. Never again. No more. And once I am gone, it *will* all be over."

"You think it will die?" said I. I suppose I sounded queer. I felt so angry at her conception of a universe that revolved around Cora Steffani. I hurried on. "And you'll disappear? Have your face remodeled, I suppose?"

"Perhaps," she said. There was a movement of her eyelids, a flaring. It was an idea. "Ollie, can't we drop the whole subject? You do mean this? I can pack?"

"You'd better," said I. "Will you need to go back to your apartment at all?" She said no, she would travel light, and she began, then and there, to organize her possessions. And I to help her.

(In fact, I searched, rather carefully, for something written down. I didn't find it.)

So there we were, two women, folding clothing, speaking of what one needs to wear, both playing the scene, nothing honest about it. She was, all the while, puzzling, wondering why I was being so very helpful, so ready to get rid of her, so easy. And I thinking to myself, I am a humbug, am I? Can't I use that?

216

"Want to pack these?" said I coming to the candy jar.

"Too heavy," she objected and put them aside.

By ten o'clock, I'd had enough. The nurses were fretting. Nothing had happened. No one had come. And I could bear no more. When I left her, she was still baffled by me.

There was nothing for me to do but go home. So I did. And I waited. No one called me. I thought bitterly that I wasn't even going to be told. But, five minutes after eleven, Charley Ives came in my door.

"What happened?" I burst.

"Nothing." He cast himself down on my sofa and begged piteously for a drink.

"Did Kent Shaw go to the Biltmore?"

"Oh yes, he went."

"Darlene?"

"No Darlene."

"What now?"

"Dunno. See if the ad runs tomorrow. Try again."

"*Why* didn't Darlene come?" I cried, impatient with that elusive character.

"Tell you, coz," said Charley, accepting liquor gratefully, "a man wants to murder her and she knows it. I don't think she is going to walk up to him in any kind of place, public or private. I don't think he'll ever lead us to Darlene Hite."

"Charley, what does 'key' mean? Is it a real key, do you think? Key to a box or something?"

"Sure. A box or something. Somewhere in New

217

York City. Or the world." Charley just looked tired. "Small matter which. I didn't find any key. Worse, he's tipped off we're watching him, I'm afraid."

"Oh me!" I said. "How?" I sat down beside him. I wanted very much to comfort him because he looked so tired and that's not like Charley Ives.

"We've corrupted the landlord, if you must know," he said. "Didn't take much to corrupt him, either. What a dump that is! So I got in, easily enough, and left the door ajar, relying on Bud's man to tip me if Shaw showed in the street. Well, some damn woman from across the hall has got to put her head in and get neighborly. Am I a friend of Kent's? An artist, am I?" Charley dared me to comment.

"Is she a friend of Kent's, do you think?" I said instead.

"I wouldn't be surprised. She looked like something out of Greenwich Village in the 'twenties."

"Couldn't you have warned her not to mention . . . ?"

"Sometimes you make your own trouble," Charley said. "To warn her might set up more importance in her mind than she will naturally give it. I don't suppose it matters. I've got a mind to grab him anyhow and stop this fooling around. Bud is right. Darlene's too smart."

"Arrest Kent Shaw?"

"We've got absolutely nothing," Charley said heavily.

"Couldn't you bluff? *Say* you've got something?"

Charley closed his eyes wearily, and with the blue

gone out of his face, it looked like something cut in age-darkened ivory.

"Charley," I said, "Cora thinks she's squeaking out of it. I gave her carfare. I told her she had a plane seat. Thinks she's skinning out of the whole business tomorrow morning."

"She won't," he said dispiritedly.

(I can't help the way my mind works.) "Look, what if Kent Shaw were to find out she's going tomorrow?" I heard myself saying. "Then, if he wants to get rid of her, I mean, *kill* her, and if he thinks she is getting away, wouldn't that stir him up, maybe?"

"And we nab him with the knife at her throat?" said Charley. "I don't want him within ten blocks of her. We can't risk losing Cora. Or any one of them. We need them *all*."

"To explain the blue envelope," I murmured. "But Charley, my boy, hope is *creative*, Marcus says. So—"

"And hope's all I've got," said he, "and that's running low. Excuse me, coz. It's restful here. A man could fall to pieces."

"Ivory Tower. I'll fill your glass," I bustled. "Where is Kent now?"

"He headed for home about ten. Bud's tucking him in. Bud will be here in a minute."

"Oh?" said I.

I brought him a freshened drink and sat down again. I didn't know what to do for him.

"Maybe I need a little sermon," said Charley. "Would you, Teacher?"

"All right," I braced myself. "Any special text?"

"Darkness before dawn? The shower that clears? Anything."

"Let us sit upon the ground," I murmured, "and tell sad stories. . . . We needn't, Charley. Marcus is *tough*. I saw it in Dr. Barron. It's not at all connected with muscles or guns or money or power. I just doubt if it's for the likes of me, or even you, to fear for *him*."

Charley said judiciously, in a moment, "Y'know, Teacher, I think you are right."

And I began to cry on Charley's shoulder.

"Cousin Ollie," said Charley, stroking my hair, "what's the matter?"

"Just because I can preach," I sobbed, "and I think I know what one *ought*, doesn't mean I *can*. I'm just a poor female, Charley, and too feeble and I never had any guts, really, and sometimes I wish somebody'd take a little pity . . ."

"Now, now," said Charley soothingly.

"I don't want to sound 'right' all the time," I wailed. "*Nobody* likes that kind of person. They ought to know that most preachy people are only preaching to themselves really because they need it so bad."

"I'm sure," Charley said gently, "anyone you'd like to like you, is going to do it." He held me off, then. "You strike me as being fairly tough, you know," he said.

"It must be a pretty good performance," I bawled.

But he wasn't going to soothe and pet me or even tease me out of it, as I supposed I hoped he would. I began to feel foolish. His face was so sad and he so rigid. "I'm *inflicting*," I snuffled. "All against my principles. Excuse me, Charley, my boy. Us old-maid school teachers get these spells. We're lone lorn creatures. I don't have a more convenient shoulder."

"Perfectly all right," said Charley. "Here he comes now, I think," he added with relief.

"Who?"

Charley was letting in Bud Gray.

Bud said, "Hi, Teacher." He didn't even notice I'd been bawling. "Bad news, tonight, eh? Well, try, try again."

"*You* don't look discouraged," I said smiling.

"Same routine tomorrow night, if the ad runs?" said Charley rather briskly. "Well, then, since I need my rest . . ."

"What's your hurry?" Bud said, surprised. So Charley hesitated. "One thing we've gained." Bud took his drink. "Kent Shaw did go to the Biltmore. Did see the ad. Did respond."

"We're 'way ahead of that, aren't we?" I said. "His being in Castine was no coincidence. Marcus says a coincidence only means that the connecting roots are underground. Am I preaching? I'm only trying to be cheerful."

Charley said with a look almost of pain, "Ollie's cheered me up. Now you cheer her up, Bud, why don't you? I am positively folding for the night."

"Cheer *her* up?" said Bud fondly. "Our little Teacher?"

Charley lifted his hand and grinned goodnight and went away. It's strange how the space between my dark walls became wider and more bare, more bleak, when he had gone.

Bud said to me, "You don't feel low, do you? Believe me, Ollie, we are going to get them."

"I believe you," I said.

"And speaking of coincidences, as you so intelligently were," (I liked Bud) "you know I thought I saw our Maine friend in the Biltmore Hotel?"

"Our who?"

"Your chaperone. May have been a relative of hers, at that. Younger get-up, that's for sure. Green whatchamacallit." He made circling motions of his forefinger around his head, "and big round jiggers from the ears. I learned one time always to look at bone structures and not hats. I sure saw a likeness." Maybe he was babbling to entertain me, because I seemed to be crying again. But I stopped that.

I said, "Oh, Bud . . . oh, Bud . . . oh, what a *fool!* Oh, Bud . . ."

"What's the matter?"

"Bones *can* be changed. *Noses* can be changed. Marcus said so. It wasn't a coincidence, not at all! Not at all!"

Bud was looking at me but soon he wasn't seeing me.

"And oh," I moaned, "I thought I was so smart. But all she did was turn out her toes and waddle and she fooled me."

"Darlene Hite," Bud said in awe.

"We *saw* her. You and I. She saved my life."

"Darlene Hite," he repeated.

"That old biddy," said I (at last), "was no Down East personally appointed chaperone for lone women at night, *at all!*"

"I think I can describe her," said Bud licking his lip, "as she is now."

"But she was in the Biltmore!" I cried. "If you saw *her* probably she saw *you*. Maybe she saw you in Maine, Bud. Maybe you scared her off tonight."

"Maybe," he said grimly. "If so, done. Never mind. I think you are right. I've got to get word out. Description. Hey, you know this can result in something?" So he kissed me a loud smack on the forehead and rushed away.

He'd been gone about five minutes when I knew where else Darlene Hite had been tonight, and might still be.

Coincidence, it was not! I began to think there was no such thing. I meant to *know*. I sat on my phone and called Charley's number. No answer. It was 11:25. He'd left about a quarter after. If he was on his way to bed, as he had said, he'd get there in another few minutes. But no answer. No answer. I couldn't reach Bud, now. I didn't have that mysterious number of theirs.

What I did . . . I called Kent Shaw. It seemed a good idea at the time.

"Kent? Olivia Hudson."

"Oh? And how's life, dear?"

"And you?" I said politely. "I thought you might like to know Cora's flying to France in the morning."

"You thought I might like to know?" he said.

"That bon voyage you promised her."

"So I did," said Kent. "Thanks very much. How early in the morning?"

"Not so early the Press won't be there," said I, "more's the pity. The flight's at nine."

"I do thank you," he said, rather shrilly. "Mustn't forget our manners, must we?"

I hung up and I thought *Oh, what have I done!* I called Charley again, in somewhat of a panic, and this time he answered.

"Charley, tell me quick," I cried, "that woman who saw you in Kent Shaw's room . . . did she wear a *green turban* and *hoop earrings?*"

"Yes."

"Then she was Darlene Hite!" It took a surprisingly short time to explain to him how this could be so. "Don't you see?" I babbled. "She's *smart*. She figured just as you did. She saw him into the Biltmore and hurried back. She wanted to get her hands on that key. She thought he'd leave it behind just as you did. Oh, Charley, has she *got* it?"

"Seems to me I was still rummaging around too close to the time he'd get in. Believe me, if she could find anything in that rat's nest, she *is* smart. Teacher, are you right, this time? The woman I saw *lives* across the hall."

"It really doesn't matter," I said, "whether I'm right. If only I *might* be, we'll have to go and see."

"I'll go see. Not you."

"Can you reach Bud?" I squirmed. I wasn't going to sit home.

"I can relay a message. He'll get it pretty fast."

"What if you don't get him, Charley?"

"So?" He sounded suspicious.

"Don't you see, you *need* me?"

"Don't you remember this Shaw is a killer and nobody for you to tangle—?"

224

"Maybe he went out. I . . . I . . . I think he has."

"What!"

"Well, I . . . I called him. I told him Cora was leaving early in the morning. Maybe he'll go . . . try for her, now. I did it to get him *away*. So we could get Darlene. Charley?"

Charley groaned. "Cousin Ollie, will you keep out of this?"

"No," I said. "I'll meet you there. You can't get along without me."

"I can't?" he said.

"I saw her in Maine and you never did, you goop!" Silence. "So, shall I pick you up, Charley, my boy?" I quavered.

"I'll be there before you, Teacher," he snapped.

So I slammed down the phone joyfully and dashed into my camel's hair coat, and ran for the elevator.

Charley, of course, first called and left the word for Bud Gray.

Then (of course) he called the hospital. He meant to alert the guards over Cora, lest Kent Shaw turn up. He couldn't risk losing *her*, for Marcus' sake.

How . . . how can I explain the things that happened that dreadful night?

CHAPTER 21

But I must try.

In the first place, consider Kent Shaw. Half mad, maybe three-quarters mad with disappointment that Darlene Hite had not kept this second rendezvous. Maybe oppressed, besides, by what he may have sensed, the watching, the searching of his room. Feeling on the verge, the absolute teetering verge of a great crashing. Then, I call and say the other bird is flying out of hand. What would Kent Shaw do but call the hospital (while Charley and I were talking) to see whether or not he had yet succeeded in getting rid of Cora Steffani?

The hospital let the call go through, on instruction, and someone listened in. So a record of that conversation exists:

"Cora, darling, I hear you are going away in the morning."

"How did you hear that, Kent, darling?"

"Oh, somebody told me. When shall I see you, to say good-by?"

"Good-by, now," Cora said to him gaily.

"But I wanted to send you a little something for bon voyage. You remember?"

226

"Mail it, Kent, dear."

"How will I know where to mail it, Cora, darling?"

"Because I will tell you," she said. "I will write. I will be gone a long time, darling, and it is possible nobody will ever see me again."

"Is that so?"

"I shall buy me a new face, don't you see? Then I won't be bothered any more. Will I?" She was gay. And she was threatening. "But of course, I can write a letter. To anyone I used to know."

"How clever of you," he said. "What an idea! I will surely mail you some token. Candy? Could I see you tonight, if I came?"

"Don't bother. I wouldn't take candy on the plane, darling, because of its weight. Although something sweet . . ."

"Mayn't I come tonight?"

"No, darling," she said rather indistinctly.

"Ah, too bad."

"It will taste as sweet, afterwards," she rumbled. "But promise not to forget."

"Oh, I swear . . ." he said.

"Help me." Silence.

Kent's ear must have been lacerated by the phone.

A nurse's voice, distantly, sharply, said, "Miss Steffani?" Then the nurse's voice, in the phone, "I'll have to hang up. I think she is fainting."

So Kent hung up and didn't think she was fainting. And no more was she. She had reached for something sweet to pop into her mouth, as they were talking.

Therefore, when Charley Ives called the hospital at

11:38, they were able to tell him that Cora seemed to have been poisoned, in some mysterious way.

Charley Ives did what he had to do. He rushed for the hospital. A dying statement could save Marcus. It was no choice really. He had to go.

Consider Bud Gray. He called that relay number, as in duty he must, and received Charley's message at 11:40. He was only five minutes away from Kent Shaw's place. The name of Darlene Hite was like a beacon. And he hurried. So, at about 11:45, Bud Gray spoke quietly to the man watching outside, and he went in. He proceeded up the stairs, heart in his mouth with hope that at last . . . at last . . .

He listened to the silence on the dingy second floor. He tapped on the door across from Kent Shaw's. Nobody answered. "Mrs. Thompson?" said Bud softly, reading from the card tacked on the door. No answer. "Mrs. Thompson, may I speak to you? Please?"

Nothing.

So Bud said, pleadingly and subtly in threat, "Darling? You'd better let me in." And again, "Darling?"

When no answer came to this either, he reluctantly retreated, to go down to the basement and roust out the landlord and get in at that door.

And now think of Kent Shaw, who must have been at first exultant. One down! One woman gone! Then, wouldn't he realize the terrible pressure that would descend now upon the other one? If Cora died, Darlene might be so terrified as to despair of the money, as to tell. Now he *must* get Darlene Hite. But how? He didn't know where she was.

228

He would have been flat against the inside of his own door, listening. He'd have heard Bud Gray say, "Darling?" And it was just as close to her name as Bud had meant it to be. In the wrong ear.

Darlene didn't answer.

Perhaps Kent cracked his door and saw Bud going away, and knew him for Charley's friend, or perhaps for what he was, a policeman. Kent would be jumpy to the point of madness, desperate to seize upon any chance whatsoever. Surely, he began to wonder what woman lived in that room, had rented it two weeks ago, and had not been seen.

Or, if he had seen her, still I had put into Cora's mind the notion of remodeling a face. And she had put the notion into his. And none of us could have known that Kent Shaw, in the course of some romantic skirmish with a former tenant, retained a key to that door.

Darlene Hite, who had boldly decided that safety was actually right across the hall from death, did not know this, either. When she heard Bud's voice, she crept from the bed, looked at the windows, turned on no light, made a mistake . . .

Consider me, knowing nothing of all this, taking a taxi, stopping it correctly three doors away. Then, hunching myself along the shadows in the correct movie-spy manner, going up the stoop, passing the man on watch who didn't know me and didn't stop me, ringing the wrong bell and getting into the house by this classic method, all the while my heart beating high with pleasurable pretending to myself that I was in danger.

I inspected the dirty cards on the downstairs wall.

One clean one said Mrs. Miles Thompson. I found Kent Shaw's name in a kind of decadently elegant script, with his room number penciled on in red. I walked up the stairs. The house smelled old and hopelessly encrusted, as if nothing could ever get it sweet and clean again.

I had only to choose the door across from Kent Shaw's. I expected Charley Ives to be there, of course. My function, as I saw it, was to lay eyes on this woman, and if she was the one from Maine, to say so. Then we could accuse and discover. At that moment, I had put aside my play-acting about danger. I three-quarters believed that Kent Shaw was not in the building. So I went blithely up and when I found the door of Darlene's room swinging, although the room had no light in it, fool that I was . . . I rushed in.

The dark hit me, as if I came up against a wall. But someone was waiting in the dark. Then, in what light came through the blind, for the dark was soon not so black, I could see a glitter, a shine. I knew him by the knife in his hand. Kent Shaw was in there waiting. I could almost sense the turmoil and the evil in his soul.

But, you see, I thought that Charley Ives was at least coming soon. I was almost sure he was already there, somewhere, and I knew that Bud would not be far behind. In the teeth of danger, I didn't even think of danger. When I saw the knife, at once I wondered if Darlene was dead. It sickened me with fear for Marcus. If Darlene was dead, if Kent had got her, and if Cora never broke and told, why then we were beaten.

So I thought I must, therefore, do something for Marcus' sake. *Somebody* had to crack and tell. Lacking Darlene there was Kent Shaw. Something must be done about him. Oh, I could have turned quickly in my tracks and gone back down the stairs but I swear that it didn't even occur to me.

By a kind of instinct that wasn't courage—for where is courage when you haven't the sense to be afraid?—I did the only thing I knew how to do. I play-acted. I jumped into another skin. Yet (because this was for my life, as I somehow also knew, as well as for Marcus)—I knew it had to be good. I had to make him *believe*. So I chose the character I'd studied for seventeen years. I became Cora Steffani.

There was no light on my face, but some light in the hall behind me. I drew myself into the high-bosomed, chin-flung-up, hip-tilted posture that was Cora. I let my hand and arm move, flowing from the shoulder, as I softly pushed the door nearer closed. Now we were in a darker place, but I had no doubt Kent Shaw could see my outline. I said in Cora's voice, "Kent, is that you, darling?"

Now you must know that the hospital was a long way uptown on the west side, whereas I'd had a straight run down from my apartment. It had taken me fourteen minutes. Oh, I didn't know that Kent had just, within minutes, called the hospital, that he knew Cora was there, poisoned, dying.

So when he said in a hoarse voice, "Darlene?" all I thought was, Ah, this is something like it! And I hoped that Charley Ives was close enough to hear.

But I couldn't play Darlene. So I said, in Cora's voice, with one of her flying movements of the hand, "No, dear. Cora. I came for what you promised."

He said, "Go away. Go back. Go back."

"But I need it, darling," said I in Cora's coaxing manner. "I'm going abroad. Didn't you know? I thought I would come for what you owe me. It's only fair." He didn't speak. I strained to *make* him speak, for evidence. "Where is Darlene?" said I, with Cora's suspicious jealousy, "have you paid her before me?"

He couldn't have been able to see my face. Of course, he did have in his mind the notion of plastic surgery. He may have expected Cora to look other than like herself, already. I knew he was confused. I didn't imagine that his masterpiece, his beautiful hoax, was turning over in his brain.

He said, "Darlene, I'm glad you are here. I'll give you the key. That's what you want, isn't it?"

But I had to stay being Cora. So I laughed Cora's high affected laughter. I wanted him to go on saying revealing and incriminating things. I thought Charley Ives had probably come on soft feet and was listening in the hall by now. I wasn't afraid. I said, "Kent, don't you know me? It's Cora Steffani, darling."

"Cora is in the hospital," he said.

"But, darling, I'm the Dream Walker—the lady you've taught so cleverly to be two places at once. . . ."

His thin shrill voice that lacked only volume to be a scream, said, "No. She got the poison. You got to be Darlene."

The word "poison" staggered me. I saw his knife lift and make ready. I'd thought, if he ran at me, to run into the hall. Now I thought, Where is Charley? I hadn't the time to be much afraid. With a vague notion that I could delay him or appease him, I said, "Oh, very well. I am Darlene."

But I couldn't play Darlene. All the negatives I was using—the voice Darlene couldn't mimic because she wasn't trained well enough, the posture that he had never been able to teach her to hold, because she hadn't the control, the gestures—these were Cora's and never Darlene's. All my wisps of knowledge had an inverted power. I had made him believe I couldn't be Darlene.

He let out a yammering sound. He cried, "Cora!" in a shriek of terror. And the knife flew at me through the air because he believed I was Cora . . . walking.

It struck me in the breastbone. I may have staggered slightly. I did not fall. I hadn't thought of his *throwing* that knife. I seemed to myself to stand there, stupidly surprised. But I stood. I knew I was alone. Charley Ives was not here. Nobody listened at the door. I had rushed in and taken the role of the victim, and nobody was going to cast me for the heroine. I thought with dumb sorrow, "Teacher, 34." Naturally, no hero . . .

The knife wasn't causing me pain. It was only dragging and heavy. But I knew Kent Shaw could, at any moment, leap and press the knife deeper and then I would die. So I stood still for my life. I said, in Cora's trill, "Why, of course. I am in the hospital, too. You can't hurt me, darling. Not now, that I've got on to the trick of being two places . . ." and I laughed Cora's laugh. So his whole design turned in his brain.

He began to whinny, a high sick sound. I knew he was afraid. I knew I could die . . . if I ran. So I took

233

a step toward the faint light that crossed under and through the flimsy blind. The knife tip was wedged, in flesh or bone, and held there. I didn't touch it. I wasn't bleeding. Kent Shaw whinnied and drew himself against the wall.

"You should keep your promises," I said reproachfully. "Darlene and I did all the work. You mustn't think you can kill us. *We* aren't Ed Jones."

He made a most horrible sound.

I shifted my course. I thought I could drive him to the window. I thought if he went through it, then I wouldn't have to die. I could see his face now. He didn't look at mine. With bursting eyeballs, he stared at the knife protruding bloodlessly from my breast bone.

"Ed Jones was mortal, Kent, darling," said I in Cora's saucy, slightly malicious voice.

He fell on the floor and rolled, out of all control, with that high whinnying sound coming steadily out of him.

The light came on. I didn't turn around because I was staring at a pair of hands that came from behind a dirty flowered curtain across the corner. The hands had a flannel sash in them and were ready to bind Kent Shaw to harmlessness. But they weren't Charley's hands.

A voice behind me said loudly, "For God's sake, Ollie!" It wasn't Charley's voice. It was Bud Gray.

He floated in two strides all the way to the corner and flung the curtain aside. He looked piercingly at the woman who had been hidden there. He took the sash out of her hands and bent and secured Kent Shaw who made no effort of any kind.

The woman said to me, "I guess he would have found me in about another minute and I left my gun in the bed. I guess you saved my life, Miss . . . Hudson, isn't it?" Her voice was not particularly nasal to my ear.

Bud said, "Sit down, Ollie. Don't touch that thing. What in hell has been going on!" He took those giant strides without waiting for an answer, and laid about him with commands, speaking to other people in the hall.

I sat down on the edge of the bed, keeping very erect, and the knife shook so I thought it might be loosened and fall of itself. I said, in my mind, Where can Charley be?

Darlene Hite, in her nightdress, stood quietly.

Bud Gray said to her, "You saved *her* life, in Maine. I think you don't like this much, any more. Am I right? Don't be afraid, Miss Darlene Hite. I've wanted to meet you for a long time. Need you on our side."

She looked at him. Her eyes fled, returned. "I've got to be, I guess," said Darlene Hite with her usual clear-headedness.

The rooming house had sprung to life all around us. I sat with the knife quivering. Darlene dressed behind the curtain, while Kent Shaw still steadily went on like a whistle that has been stuck open and the noise begins to rub on the raw of one's nerves. Then police came and soon the ambulance, and a cool and imperturbable young man pulled that knife away. And Bud Gray watched Darlene with glowing eyes and talked and slowly she seemed to respond, to go toward him. So there I was, very numb and calm, sitting with my blouse in tatters and nothing but a wad of gauze to make me decent, when finally Charley Ives walked in.

His face was stone. His eyes were porcelain.

"My hero!" said I, idiotically. "What kept you?"

I saw his eyes blaze and, dizzy with a great revealing sense of utter relief . . . I fainted.

Dr. Harper said, "That wound's not much. You're all right, Olivia." I was in the emergency room at the hospital. He was better than reassuring. He let me talk and sort out my own impressions of the immediate past. I finally got what I was afraid to ask out of my mouth. "Cora?"

"Worst possible place to try any poisoning is a first-class hospital," the doctor said complacently. "We got at her with everything in the book. Cora's all right."

"How did it happen?"

"Candies. Humbugs, they call 'em." I let out a startled wail. "How the devil they got to her we still don't know," he said.

"Is she telling . . . ?"

"She couldn't very well talk while we worked on her, believe me. She's back in her bed, playing too sick to speak, thinking it over, I suppose. Charley Ives is fit to be tied."

"He was *here*, then?"

"Hanging over her, with a tape-recorder running."

"*Of course*," said I. "Did they bring Kent Shaw here?"

The doctor shook his head. I didn't like what I saw in his eyes. "Sit up. You're fine. You're also lucky. I better see if Charley's around."

A nurse was helping me put my clothing back together over the bandages when Charley came bursting in. He cast one glance at me and my latest immodesty. The bright blue of his eye was not exactly sympathetic. He spoke briefly to the doctor. He marched over. I understood.

I burst into apology. "Oh, Charley, I was *wrong*. And *you* were right. I shouldn't have done anything I did."

"True," Charley said gently but firmly.

"And you *had* to be with Cora. I didn't mean to reproach you. I was just scared, Charley."

Charley blinked. His face turned wooden.

"Is he really clear out of his head? Kent Shaw?" I cried. "So nothing he says can be evidence? Charley, is it that bad?"

"He's pretty much gone," Charley said.

"Then, I've wrecked everything."

"Anything could have sent him off the deep end," Charley said impatiently. "Don't beat yourself, now. Darlene thinks she'd have been gone . . ." Then he relaxed and looked amused. "You know, a little ordinary human cowardice, and you could have yelled for help. Bud was in the basement."

"Oh," said I stupidly, "then I had a hero after all." Thunderous silence. "I'm sorry for what I said," I was nearly bawling. "For what I did . . . everything . . ."

"Never mind, coz. Bud has Darlene. But why he didn't jump a little faster into that room I'll never . . ."

"Oh no, Bud was wonderful," said I, thinking of Darlene and how Bud had projected to her, somehow, in those impossible circumstances, his friendliness and his admiration and his hope for her. "But it's all right," I cried, feeling reprieved, "if Darlene is talking."

Charley said, "It'll be all right," in a manner just a little too soothing.

I was alarmed all over again. All I could think was that I'd hurt Marcus. "Charley, if Bud was there soon enough to hear what was said, how Kent kept calling me Darlene, and all that . . . won't it help?"

"We've got Kent Shaw," said Charley. "Don't worry about that."

"And Cora?"

"Uh huh," he said. "So now you get home to bed. Walking around with knives . . . of all the . . . !" He turned his back abruptly. "Bud said it was a top performance, in fact, it fooled *him*. Had enough, coz? Better go home, hadn't you?"

"Charley, my boy," said I tartly, "you're a lousy actor. I've said so before. What I did is even worse than I know, isn't it? Tell Teacher, come on."

Charley turned around again. "Okay, Teacher," he sighed. "It's this way. Kent Shaw is in no shape to tell us how he put the blue envelope in the book. Darlene doesn't know anything about that. She wasn't coached about Washington. She wasn't there. And *she* can't tie in Pankerman. She never heard of his being in it. Now, lacking Kent Shaw, only Raymond Pankerman can tell us about the blue envelope, since he wrote the letter that was in it, and he must have given it to Shaw. The problem is, get Pankerman. Him and his Fifth Amendment."

"But Cora can tie in Pankerman," I said slowly, "can't she? She'd know Kent Shaw had no money. And she'd make sure where the money was coming from."

"I should think so, too. But you see, Cora isn't talking. Yet."

"But you've *got* her. For Heaven's *sakes*, Charley!"

"Sure. Sure, we've got her."

"Don't you think you can make her talk?"

Charley said with false cheer, "Maybe. Maybe I'm just pessimistic." We looked at each other. There was that hard stubborn fight in Cora, that long practiced clawing and scratching for her advantage. There would be no repentance, no aching conscience, no intolerable pain of guilt, to break her down. She didn't even understand what, indeed, she had done.

"Bud's got Darlene upstairs, now. Going to try. We're waiting on the Boss," Charley told me. "We can tell her we've got Kent Shaw."

"She doesn't know . . . how he is?"

"No."

"But you haven't got him," I said sadly, "because Kent Shaw *isn't*, any more. Will he recover in time, Charley?"

Charley just shook his head.

"Then," I said, "it's not going to be easy to make Cora talk." And then I saw headlines, pictures, heard arguments . . . and I could see months and months of it, and Cora cast as the lone, the under-dog . . . and some woolly-headed sympathy edging around . . . and a long, noisy, damaging struggle yet before us. Unless she confessed, too.

"You don't have leverage," I said, "and she's got nothing to lose."

Charley sat down suddenly on a chair next to mine and he took my hands. "Coz, do you know how to make her talk?" I shook my head. "I forced you to try acting my way," he said. "Maybe I don't understand . . ."

"I . . . I did have a silly idea," I said. "It's wild and foolish. It's only play-acting."

"We've got to have her story. If we can't smash all of it, in one blow . . ."

"I know," I said.

"*I* don't know how to deal with her. I've made nothing but mistakes since I met her. Thought I found something I'd been missing—gaiety, spice of life. Ran into something too tortuous and unprincipled for . . . well, for me. Tried to get out of it and made a mess of that, too. I can make her angry, coz. But I'm never the one to know how to make her talk." Charley frightened me, being as humble as this.

"Unless," I said, "you touch a feeling that's true, you won't do it."

"She hasn't any feelings," he said bitterly.

"Yes. She has," I said.

"Coz?" Charley seemed to be listening hard as he could to my very thoughts. "Had you better come along upstairs?"

The doctor said, "Now, just a minute. She's had about enough for one night. Came damned close to being killed."

"Twice over," I said. "She offered me a piece of
240

candy and I was too stupid to ask where it came from."

Charley said to me sternly, "No good to Marcus, for you to bewail how stupid you are."

"Why, that's so," said I, bracing up.

"If you even think you've got the least idea how to help."

I felt better, suddenly. "Wait and see," I said, "and if she's too tortuous for you . . ." I suppose I grinned.

"Uh huh," said Charley, sounding more cheerful. "Takes fire to fight fire. You better tag along. What will you *do?*" he demanded.

"Nothing, I hope. If I have to, I'll . . . tell her some truth." (I knew I had to say this.) "She'll never *believe,* unless I do, you know."

Charley said under his breath, "Teacher, you terrify me."

"Let me go," I said, "in a wheel chair, I think." I looked down at my blouse which was blood-stained. "Just as I am."

"Hold on to your hat, Doc," said Charley Ives grimly.

CHAPTER 22

They pushed me, in a wheel chair, down the familiar corridor on the 8th floor and into Cora's room, where there was a crowd. She was lying abed, pale, her lids languorous. They lifted at sight of me. "Why, Ollie?" she whimpered in surprise.

I made *my* lids languorous and sick, and said nothing, laying foundations.

"What happened?" she asked weakly.

Nobody answered her. A man I'd never seen before said quietly, "All in order? Shall we begin?" He was a stocky individual with very large eyes over which flesh, beneath his brows, seemed to fall in a fold. Bud Gray was standing near him, exuding a kind of possessiveness over Darlene Hite, in the easy chair. Her almost white, very pale, hair, was caught back neatly. Her gray eyes were serious. Her hands were quiet. Her attitude was subdued and businesslike. Yet I could imagine that something about her was leaning, leaning with pitiable relief and trust, on Mr. Horace (Bud) Gray. They made a pair. I saw Ned Dancer being a mouse in the corner with his ears out.

Cora's black-and-yellow robe was thrown around her shoulders and the long folds, that should fall to her feet, lay like a long splash above the white coverlet. She was keeping still, in seventeen languages. Oh, I knew her! I prayed I knew her, now. Her eyes disdained Darlene Hite, skipped over Charley with a flicker of scorn, but when they shifted to me they were not satisfied.

I touched the floor with my toe and rolled the chair ever so slightly that light might fall on my bandages and my blood.

The Boss began, in a cold monotone, to outline the plot. He began to ring in Darlene's testimony, by his questions and her answers, her firm precise, untinted answers. It rolled out, sounding complete and damning.

Finally he said, "Now you had a certain written memorandum of all this, Miss Hite. The times, places, and the words you were to say?"

"I did." Her voice was untrained, to be sure, but the nasal quality was really very slight and it was not unpleasant.

"You have it still?" she was asked.

"I have only the instructions for Castine. The others I burned. It is in a kind of shorthand but I can read it for you."

"You think Miss Steffani had a duplicate?"

"Yes, sir."

"May we see yours?"

Darlene took a pair of eyeglasses out of her bag. They were hung on a cord by means of short rubber tubes slipped over the earpieces, just as Cora's also were. Darlene pulled off one of the rubber tubes and produced from its interior a tiny scrap of paper.

Bud Gray now raised his hands and we saw that he had Cora's glasses. He did as Darlene had done. But there was nothing hidden, nothing there. Cora had managed to destroy it all. Her mouth twitched.

Charley Ives said, "No matter."

The Boss said, "That about tells the story. We will move into court. Miss Hite can give her side of it. Raymond Pankerman is available. Kent Shaw is in custody."

Cora said, "Am I in custody?"

"You are."

"Then, I am," she said and shrugged. (I almost saw her legs crossing on some witness stand.)

Charley tried very hard to look relieved. "Pretty clever," he drawled. "Why don't you tell us your side of it, Cora?"

Cora said, "Why should I tell you anything? You all think you know everything." Her eyes jerked to me. "What happened to Ollie?" she asked irritably.

I said, broodingly, "Kent Shaw and I disagreed, that's all."

Cora bit her lip. Her eyes traveled from side to side. She was shrewd. She leaned back. "Well," she said petulantly, "I should think the doctor might explain that I ought to be asleep. I was *poisoned*, you know."

"I know," I murmured. (It puzzled her.)

"I'm ready to take down anything you have to say," said Bud Gray. (Dancer was, too.)

"Why, bless you," said Cora impudently. "Then, take down this. That woman doesn't look one bit like me. You say she's had an operation. *I* say she just wants in on my publicity."

Charley said, "Won't do, Cora."

"No?" said Cora. "Where is Kent Shaw? That pip-squeak mastermind. Why haven't you got *him* here?" Oh, she was shrewd.

"They are examining him downtown," Charley lied, placidly.

"Where?" said Cora. "In the morgue? Ah, ah, mustn't fib, you know. If Ollie got hurt as bad as that, surely she was well avenged by all these big strong men." I heard the malice and the jealousy in that tone. "I'd sure like to know what happened to the other fellow," she said, looking incorrigibly saucy.

"He isn't dead," Charley said. "Don't make that mistake."

"Then, bring him around, why don't you?" she challenged.

If she knew Kent Shaw was insane, and unable to bear witness, we might never get the truth about the blue envelope and without that one detail . . . Now, she'd got in her head the notion that Kent Shaw was dead, and no witness, ever. No danger. So Cora was going to hang on. She had to. Guilt didn't bother her and good-looking women had got off things before. She could be very confusing. It was her only chance. In a muddle she might squeak through. She had nothing to lose by trying. She wasn't going to confess. I stopped hoping for it.

"Tell us about Pankerman," the Boss said, as if she gladly would. The suggestion of his manner didn't work.

"I've seen his name in the papers," said Cora. "Is that what you mean?" Her eyes lit with the old mis-

245

chief. "Oh go on, it's nothing but a plot," said Cora outrageously. "To save your precious John Paul Marcus from what are his just deserts, as far as I can see. I don't care what you say or do. Keep me in custody. *I dream. That's all I know.*" She sighed prettily. "More headlines," she pouted. "Will I always be the most famous woman in America?"

Several people in that room (including me) could have socked her. There she was, Cora Steffani, phony, illogical, unreasonable . . . completely beaten, and still not beaten. And what was there to do?

Darlene Hite frowned faintly and looked up at Bud Gray. Gray looked at Charley Ives. Charley turned his head, ever so slightly. Before he could turn too obviously to me, I knew I was for it. I said, deep in my throat, "Too much ham in me, after all."

They all looked at me. Ned Dancer's neck stretched.

"Most famous woman in America," I began to laugh. I arched my back which I hoped would make the blood flow from my little wound. I put my fingers on the bandage and drew them away and looked at them, as if there were blood. "Changed my mind," I said. "I don't think I'll take this secret to the grave." I looked insolent. I felt power. (Oh, there is nothing like a Bad Girl role. It's so comparatively simple and easy.)

The doctor looked startled and moved and I said sharply, "No, Doctor. If I want to sing a swan-song, I shall do it. This is a fine audience, as good as I'd choose."

(Charley had to help me. I had to make him help

246

me.) I glanced at Cora only briefly. "Old friend, dear friend," I said, and laughed. "You'll only be the second most famous woman in America, tomorrow morning."

"What are you talking about?" said Charley, almost too hopefully.

"So many men in the world," I said to him, "why did I want only you?" I sultried my eyes. (Oh, it's corny. It's easy.) And Charley was staring at me. "You should know, gentlemen," said I, "for future reference, that a woman who wants a certain man very much, and cannot get him, really has to protect herself." I looked only at Charley.

Did Cora wince?

"It's a weird triangle," said I, "that's only two parallel lines. I thought you were fond of your wife." I bit that word out, looking at Charley, for this was necessary. And he did what I wanted. He locked his gaze with mine. "Charley, my boy," said I and it wasn't teasing, "can you imagine? Cora thought you were fond of *me?* But Charley Ives isn't fond of any woman, is he? And long ago the old man," I said viciously, "didn't hold with cousins marrying."

I could feel Cora's stare.

"Women are dangerous," I said. "Aren't we, Cora?" I didn't turn my head.

"What are you raving about?" she exploded. I did *not* look at her.

Neither did Charley. He kept taut the line of attention between us two.

"It's been amusing," I said. "You thought she was using me, didn't you, Charley? When *I've* used Kent

247

Shaw. *I've* used Ray Pankerman. *I've* used my old friend Cora. *I'm* the one with the money," I said contemptuously.

People were shocked and silent. I smiled in insolent power. "Don't you believe it? Why, how funny! How very amusing! How is it that nobody wonders why Kent Shaw went after *me* with his knife? Little man, loved his little part, he did. Couldn't even trust *me* not to tell." My eyes clung to Charley's eyes. I tried to pierce him with a look of meanness and power. His face was slowly turning red and horrified. "But now I tell because I choose," I said haughtily. "Let it smash. I'd like to have killed your ex-wife, Charley, my boy. I could do without her. Such a witty way to do it, too. With a humbug. Oh, if I had and if Kent hadn't been quite so quick . . . But I don't mind," said I. "It would have been very dull."

I threw back my head and strangled my voice with tension and ugliness. "Two places at once! Wasn't it *fun?* And you're not very happy. You hate her, now. And me, too? Then so much for True Love, Charley, my boy." I leaned forward. "Still, now that you know what I did, in my Ivory Tower, *that I pulled all the strings*, will you call me Teacher for this lesson?"

And Charley said, in a frightened voice, "Cousin Ollie!"

So I let it all go. I let my heart break. I said, "Charley, I've been . . . hurt . . . so long. You didn't care. *Did* you? Charley?" I fell back.

Charley flew to me, knelt to me. I put my hand, my fingers spread, on the back of his head, in his hair.

Cora had her legs curled under her and was on her

knees. "That's just not *so*," she gasped, childishly. "That's not *so*." She beat her fists and howled for attention. "It wasn't her money. She hasn't got that kind of money. I can prove it was Pankerman's. Kent and I watched him put it in the safe. I think she's gone crazy. Make her tell you," screamed Cora Steffani, "that she's just a liar!"

"Where is this safe?" said Bud Gray quickly, softly.

She told them where it was. She began to tell them everything.

"Get me out of here," I said in Charley's ear. So he signaled and the doctor wheeled me out.

In the corridor I got stiffly out of the chair. "You said I can go home? This isn't so bad I have to stay here?"

"No, no, go home if you want to." The doctor was looking at me with a blank expression.

Ned Dancer came out. I was standing, calm and collected. He stopped in his tracks and said sourly, "Quite an act."

"Only way I could think of," I told him. "She was going to cause too much trouble. The one thing she couldn't stand was to think *I'd* fooled her."

"Should auld acquaintance be forgot," said Ned, surprising me with such quick understanding.

Dr. Harper said with a very phony laugh, "You pretty near fooled me, I can tell you."

Charley Ives came flying out of Cora's room. He shot blue lightning at Ned, who said, quickly, "I won't use it. Couldn't hope to." Then, like a male, "Dames, huh?"

"Takes a dame to fight a dame," said Charley heartily. "Cora's tied in Pankerman all right. And she says Kent Shaw gave her the title of that book in March. In a ladies' room, for gosh sakes. So we've got it!"

"That's splendid," said I, stiffly.

He took me by the shoulders. "Wow!" He was grinning. (I didn't think he was fooled, somehow.)

"It was a real juicy part, and very melo," I said in my teacher's voice, "but, you see, it was sound."

"Sound?" Now Charley sounded strange.

"The feeling. I told you. It was *hers*. Her own true feeling. The meanest kind of jealousy. So she was afraid what I said *might* be so, because she recognized the *feeling*. That's about the only thing can make-believe. See Dramatics 2, Miss Hudson, Monday, Wednesday and Friday."

Charley looked queer. He let me go.

"But you mustn't worry," I said primly. "It wasn't *all* because she felt things about you. Or about me. She had several other motives mixed in."

"I . . . daresay," he drawled. "I'll try to be tough about it."

I heard myself snap, "Now, if you think you can manage, I'd like to go home."

He said, wryly, "Teacher, we can always call you. . . ."

Ned Dancer was gone.

"Oh, Charley," I said, "I suppose you thought I was off my rocker. But you can't act and so I *had* to. I'm glad if it worked. I hope you understand. I bet you don't."

(I guess he understood.)

"Rest your imagination," Charley said kindly and kissed me in a fond cousinly way and sent me home.

CHAPTER 23

The whole thing burst with one last bang. How quickly it died away! What's duller than a burst balloon? People, on the whole, got that one word. *Hoax.* They then said, if they could, "I told you so." And if they couldn't, they said, and still say, darkly, "There's a lot more we haven't been told."

Kent Shaw went to a mental hospital. Ray Pankerman collapsed. Wept useless dollar signs. As much money as they found in that safe can't travel without leaving traces. He even asked for Marcus' mercy, in confessing about the blue envelope. But the law had *him.*

The law would have to examine the murder of Ed Jones. Was Cora an accessory? Was Darlene? Then, it would all roll out under the rules, and the evidence be presented exhaustively. Millions would be too bored to read every question and answer, or to reason and conclude from these, or take the pains. Yet there, in the questions and answers, would be every careful detail, the very best we could do.

Marcus' household was happier and Marcus on the phone was just the same. Vindicated as far as was humanly possible. But he has a scar.

My wound healed nicely. It wasn't much. I stayed at

home and talked as freely as I could to all newsmen, all callers. Miss Reynolds had asked me back, since I now began to rank as a clever spy on the right side. The girls came by and made a fuss of me. Oh, I'd go back. When summer was over.

Meantime, I had no work. I felt empty. All my friends came to see me, but no Cora Steffani, and I missed her like an aching tooth. The pain of that was still in me, the echoes of all the years of tension between us, an occupation lost, in a victory that left me empty. I was let-down. I felt like a fool, besides. I was really moping. I didn't go to Washington.

A week had gone by. It was late, the night he came.

"Didn't want to run into a mob, here," he told me. "Have I timed it right?"

"Everybody's gone home, Charley, my boy," said I brightly. "I was about to go to bed, myself. Tell me, how is Marcus?"

"Marcus is fine. Tough, you know." Charley sat down. My walls bulged, as ever they did when he came in. "And you?" asked he.

"Nothing left but an interesting little scar," I said and hurried on, wishing I hadn't put it quite that way. "I'm doing business at the old stand. Back to school in the fall. All is forgiven."

"Splendid," he drawled.

"Where is Darlene Hite?" I asked quickly. "Vanished again? I don't read about her."

"Bud doesn't want her read about. She's in Washington, under his wing. He's fighting to save her, says she's too valuable to be sacrificed, cites theories of modern penology, wants her free and working for him.

252

I'll bet he's going to win. Besides being smart, she's quite a fine girl, or can be."

"Bud always was entranced by Darlene Hite," said I, amused. "I think he fell in love with her modus operandi."

Charley threw back his head and roared.

"It wasn't *that* funny," I said feebly. I was uncomfortable. I knew, whatever I did, I could put on no act for *myself,* any more. "Charley, my boy," I said, "if you will excuse me and come again another day? Us teachers retire pretty early."

"Stop that!" said Charley Ives violently.

"What?"

"I'll be damned if I'll let you pull that Teacher stuff, ever again. You've intimidated me long enough."

"I . . . ?"

"Sit still, and I mean still." (I sat still.) "I am going to tell you some things Marcus said. I—seems, I repeated your remark about you and Cora being measuring-sticks. Marcus says that's *so*. He says people do that for each other. He says"—Charley looked at me nervously.

"You and I had a fight," he stated, starting all over again.

"We did, indeed. We still fight. We *may,* any minute," I said primly.

"*Exactly,*" pounced Charley. "Now, Marcus says you were once a moonstruck little girl, thin-skinned, sensitive, timid."

"I—I am."

"Marcus says you *were*. But now, he says, you have courage, you have bite and force, and a sense of duty

253

as big as you are, because what I said, on my side of that fight, has rankled all this time."

"Oh, I don't . . ." I stammered. "I can't . . . I'm certainly not all that."

"As for me," said Charley, swelling up. "I was pretty crude. A narrow violent type, hell-bent, slam-bang, and on my way to being the kind who shoots first and asks questions, if any, afterwards. But now he says, I can see grays, and I've become sensitive and I may even grow up, someday. Because I've brooded many hours on what you said. So, Marcus says, people sometimes are each other's measuring-sticks," Charley turned his eyes, "in envy and antagonism, or else in love."

I could not breathe. I sat still.

"So I think," Charley said awkwardly, "you really are my Teacher."

"Then," said I, and our eyes locked, "you are mine."

"That's so," said he quietly.

I trembled.

"Am I a mouse?" said Charley Ives to the wall, "or a cat to look at the Queen? To hang around Cora's apartment because my cousin Ollie loyally wouldn't have anything to do with me, but she did come there. And then get struck with the notion that you and Bud Gray . . ."

"Charley, my . . ."

"Stop that!"

"Charles," I said. But oh, I was warm and my blood was flowing and the world was alive and I was in the fray. "Are you trying to figure out whether we are in love with each other?"

"I am," he said. "And oh, my not-so-very-much-a-cousin Ollie, my apostle of gentle kindness and wildest melodrama, my tigercat with a touchy conscience, my bold, ridiculous, adorable, terrifying little Teacher," his fingers touched my chin, *"wasn't* it true, Love?"

I told him how true it was, without a word.

The End.

Ah, finished, and with a clinch, too! What a mess I've made of it! Haven't put in that Pankerman's in jail, that Cora got off with a short sentence and is now abroad and God knows how she lives. That Kent Shaw is still in his limbo. That Darlene Hite has "vanished" although I know Bud Gray knows where she is and what she is doing. Oh well, all this must go in somewhere.

But *I* won't do it. Haven't time. I'll look at Portugal on the ceiling and it won't be long. I can tell.

Be born, child. I am not afraid. Dr. Harper's an old fuss-budget and Charley is a thousand times worse. Putting me here in the hospital weeks early! As if I, only thirty-five years old, can't quite safely bear this child! Never did it before, but Dr. Barron, when he married us, wished us a dozen.

Boy? Call him Charley? For my husband, my lover, my darling, my foe . . .

Secretary. You, girl. Delete this. Stop where I said "The End." Mind, now!

OLIVIA HUDSON IVES

Nurse?

EDITOR TO PUBLISHER:

How about the beginning and ending, Charley?

G.D.

PUBLISHER TO EDITOR:

Leave it the way it is, George. I've got a daughter who'll eat it up when she gets to the romantic age. I'm bound she'll have it. Never mind what her Mama says. I'll fight for this.

C.I.

THE END